GIRL FOUND

A DETECTIVE KAITLYN CARR MYSTERY

KATE GABLE

BYRD BOOKS LLC

COPYRIGHT

Visit my website at www.kategable.com

WANT TO BE THE FIRST TO KNOW ABOUT MY UPCOMING SALES, NEW RELEASES AND EXCLUSIVE GIVEAWAYS?

Sign up for my newsletter:
https://www.subscribepage.com/kategableviplist

Join my Facebook Group:
https://www.facebook.com/groups/833851020557518

Bonus Points: Follow me on BookBub and Goodreads!

https://www.goodreads.com/author/show/
21534224.Kate_Gable

ABOUT KATE GABLE

Kate Gable loves a good mystery that is full of suspense. She grew up devouring psychological thrillers and crime novels as well as movies, tv shows and true crime.

Her favorite stories are the ones that are centered on families with lots of secrets and lies as well as many twists and turns. Her novels have elements of psychological suspense, thriller, mystery and romance.

Kate Gable lives in Southern California with her husband, son, a dog and a cat. She has spent more than twenty years in this area and finds inspiration from its cities, canyons, deserts, and small mountain towns.

Write her here:

Kate@kategable.com

Check out her books here:

www.kategable.com

Sign up for my newsletter:
https://www.subscribepage.com/kategableviplist

Join my Facebook Group:
https://www.facebook.com/groups/833851020557518

Bonus Points: Follow me on BookBub and Goodreads!

https://www.bookbub.com/authors/kate-gable

https://www.goodreads.com/author/show/
21534224.Kate_Gable

amazon.com/Kate-Gable/e/B095XFCLL7

facebook.com/kategablebooks

bookbub.com/authors/kate-gable

instagram.com/kategablebooks

ALSO BY KATE GABLE

All books are available at ALL major retailers! If you can't find it, please email me at
kate@kategable.com

Girl Missing (Book 1)

Girl Lost (Book 2)

Girl Found (Book 3)

Girl Taken (Book 4)

Girl Hidden (FREE Novella)

ABOUT GIRL FOUND

While her missing sister's case goes cold, Detective Kaitlyn Carr searches for a US Marine who has disappeared after a college student is found dead in his apartment.

Where is he? Did he kill her and run? And if so, why? **Detective Kaitlyn Carr will stop at nothing to find out what happened.**

The marine's father is certain that his son would never do anything to harm his friend. That's why he reported the murder and is doing his best to help Kaitlyn find his son. But will this be a regret that will haunt him for the rest of his life?

Back in her hometown of Big Bear Lake, Violet's disappearance is running out of clues. Everyone has been interviewed. All leads have been followed up on. Now what? Kaitlyn keeps trying. She can't give up.

Will Kaitlyn find out who killed the girl and find the marine before there's another murder?

Will Kaitlyn be able to find another lead to keep her sister's case open?

Girl Found is a suspenseful thriller perfect for fans of A. J. Rivers, Mary Stone, Willow Rose, James Patterson, Melinda Leigh, Kendra Elliot, Ella Gray, and Karin Slaughter. It has mystery, angst, a bit of romance and family drama.

1

They found Violet's clothes last night rolled up in a bag consisting of everything that she wore the night of her disappearance: her shirt, her jeans, her bra, her underwear, her necklace, her socks, her shoes.

They found the bag of her things but not Violet herself.

The clothing was found in a bag under a fallen tree tied up and carefully hidden by someone on purpose.

Why? Why did they take her, my sweet, kind, beautiful, thirteen-year-old sister named for the color of eyes that she had always wanted to have?

It has been days since anyone has seen her. Being a detective, I know as well as anyone that we might not be looking for her anymore. We're looking for her body.

"They found them about a mile away from the observatory," Luke Gavinson tells me as my whole body starts to shake.

He's speaking loudly into the phone, but he sounds like he's miles away. It's like my ears are plugged with something cotton, wax, earbuds. All I hear is a thumping of my own blood and the steady sound of my heartbeat speeding up.

"The Observatory?" I ask even though I know fully well what he means.

There's a big white structure with a telescope across the lake from the house where I grew up, where Violet was living with my mom. I've never been inside the observatory itself, but the park is popular with teenagers and visitors. There's a beautiful hiking and biking path nearby through the meadow and a protected marshland for the fish and the birds.

"I'll be there as soon as I can," I say, but Luke stops me.

"No, that's not a good idea. You're driving back and forth. It's three hours each way and you're just exhausting yourself. Besides..." Luke's voice drops off.

I know what he's going to say. I had just had an encounter with an armed suspect. He wants me to take some time off.

He wants me to relax. He's worried about me, not just on a professional level, but on a personal one.

What I'm worried about is the fact that there's a second girl who's missing from Violet's school, disappearing under very similar circumstances. What I'm worried about is the fact that the situation has become dire enough for the FBI to be called in for help.

That's why he's there. Luke's not there as a personal favor to me, not at all. He's there because the FBI thinks that they need to get involved and that's both a positive and a negative.

I'm glad he's there. I'm happy that there are now the resources of the FBI at Violet's disposal looking for her. I'm also terrified. It has been days and with each passing hour, Violet will be harder and harder to find.

I tell him that I'll be there soon, but he cuts me off again.

"Listen, I know that you want to be here and I do, too, but there's nothing you can do. You don't have any jurisdiction here."

"What are you talking about? I have to look for my sister. People talk to me because I'm a detective."

"I know, but you have already asked a lot of people questions. You have done a lot."

"Not enough." I dig my heels in.

"You need to take some time off. Okay? Not long. I just mean don't drive up here right now."

"When? When would be an appropriate time for me to look for my sister?" I ask sarcastically.

"Don't be like that," Luke says. "Please, you know that what I'm saying is right. You know that I'm just looking out for you."

"I don't need anyone to look out for me. Okay? Least of all you."

"What is that supposed to mean?"

I clench my jaw. I didn't want to get into this right now. I don't really want to get into this at all, but I can't help what I think and feel every time I talk to him. There's still so much that has been left unsaid, but this isn't the right time to address that.

"You know that they're just processing the scene, Kaitlyn. They just found the bag and we don't know what else we're going to find. The crime scene technicians are here. They have everything set up, but it's going to be hours. Okay? It's going to take a while for it all to be collected, let alone processed in a lab."

"What about Neil?" I ask. "He's the last person to see her, remember?"

Neil Goss is Violet's middle school friend. He had come up to my mom and confessed to both of us that they had made plans to see each other the night that she had disappeared.

They met up right after Kaylee dropped her off and they went to the observatory, made out, and did God knows what else. He didn't admit to anything beyond that. He was distraught and upset, but he didn't have to come forward. I know all of these things, but I also know that he has to be hiding something.

He told us all of that to cover his tracks. He told us that to place himself at the scene and to explain why he was there because he suspects that we are about to find something.

"You cannot talk to Neil again. Neither of us can. Captain Talarico was very clear about that. He's in charge of the investigation and if Neil talks to us again, which I highly doubt, given who his father is, we are going to do it in a controlled environment with cameras to record exactly what he says."

Luke doesn't tell me anything that I don't already know. Of course, it has to be this way.

We have to build a case.

The thing that I think everyone seems to be forgetting here is that Violet is not dead. No bodyhas been found and there is no confirmation that she was killed. That means that there's still a possibility of her being alive.

"Okay, fine," I agree. "You keep me updated about anything else that you find. Okay? I have to go into work and do some more paperwork anyway. Please, promise me that you'll let me know if you find anything else, however insignificant."

He promises, but he knows very well that even though that's what I made him promise, what I'm actually asking him is that I'll be his first phone call if or when they find her body.

Uncertain as to what to do when I'm not working, given the fact that I don't have kids or a husband, I go into the office, sit down at my desk, and start to fill out reports about the last case that I worked on.

I take a few little breaks to get a cup of coffee here and there, but mostly I work. I know that this is not the typical existence of a woman my age, but I don't mind.

I've never really wanted children or imagined myself with a child, but I have been thinking about getting a pet. Unfortunately, my schedule is so erratic and unpredictable that I know that it will be highly unfair to have my dog or cat wait for me dutifully at home while I work twelve, fifteen, or eighteen-hour days, whatever the job requires.

I'm a workaholic in the truest sense of the word. I don't have anything else going on. I don't even have any hobbies.

This is what I sink my time into.

I work on cases well after others have given up. I work on cases well after they go cold. I think about them, even though the files and the boxes of folders have been put away.

I've solved a few mainly because I refused to give up.

I'm tenacious and that's admired in the department in general, except that personally, I know that I'm an addict.

My addiction is not alcohol, drugs, or partying like it is for many of my colleagues.

No, it's just work.

After I had to use a weapon to protect myself, I started seeing the court appointed psychologist to help me deal with my issues. All cops dread these interactions. We worry about being written up and analyzed and then demoted or passed over for promotions, but the woman I've started seeing has actually put my mind at ease. I like talking to her and she has told me a number of things that make a lot of sense.

I'm a workaholic because I'd rather spend my time working than living. Usually this affliction affects men because women can find solace and meaning in their children and in the children's activities, but in my case, I like to bury my head in my work.

It gives me peace.

It distracts me from my life and all of the disappointments and sadness that I have experienced way before my sister's disappearance.

2

Before Violet went missing, I actually considered getting a hobby. I've always enjoyed writing, even dabbled in a short story here and there. It's not a completely unknown thing for a detective to retire and start writing crime fiction.

Why couldn't that be me? I even started a few novels, started but never finished.

I open my laptop, click over to the hidden folder, and read over the 2,000 words on the screen.

I haven't looked at it for quite some time and it immediately takes me away.

"It's not at all bad," I say to myself, nodding my head.

I finish my cup of coffee and switch over to tea. If I have too much coffee, I get jittery and have a hard time falling asleep, but the mellow mint tea with no caffeine does little to calm my jitters.

It's almost time for lunch, but instead of going downstairs, I just head to the vending machine and grab a pack of pretzels. I'm a pretzel junkie, though they're probably just as bad for me as potato chips.

I pop one into my mouth one after another and crunch my teeth. I open the second story, which I had started working on when I had a little bit of downtime. I put my fingers to the keyboard to add a sentence when a call comes in.

They need a detective to go to an apartment building near Sunset Avenue.

A body has been found.

A sigh of relief washes over me. I'm the next detective in line, but as soon as I grab my bag and start to head toward the elevators, Captain Medvil stops me.

"No," he says, picking up the receiver. "I'm sending someone else."

"It's my turn."

"Doesn't matter. You need some time off."

"Absolutely not." I shake my head, taking a step closer to him.

He lowers the receiver and stares at me. He narrows his eyes and adjusts his big stance. He's got broad shoulders and a wide face with a typical short haircut favored by cops.

"I'm next on the rotation," I say. "This is my case."

"I get to decide who gets what case. I'm the captain, remember? How are you feeling?"

"Fine," I say quickly, a little bit too quickly and he tilts his head, showing his disbelief.

"No, I'm seriously fine. Okay?"

"That was kind of a scary situation. You shouldn't have been there alone like that."

"Okay. That's over," I say, waving my hand.

"What about your sister? Any news?"

I know fully well that he can find out the truth with one phone call if he suspects that I'm lying or obfuscating something.

Then he'll never let me live it down.

"They found her clothes in a plastic bag under a tree."

"Her clothes?" he asks.

"Yeah, no blood. No body. They're not ripped. Just all of her clothes."

"What do you mean?" he asks.

"I don't know. I guess someone had her change out of them for some reason."

"Her underwear as well?"

"Yeah. Socks and shoes, everything. Even her necklace. The FBI is investigating it. They're processing the scene right now."

"So why aren't you rushing over there to be a part of it?" he asks, folding his arms across his chest.

I shake my head.

"Did Captain Talarico tell you to stay away because you were interfering with the investigation?" he asks, tilting his head and saying it slowly with great accentuation to drive his point home.

It's not technically my jurisdiction. Actually, it's not my jurisdiction there at all.

I'm just the sister of the missing girl, but I've been investigating and asking questions as if I were a detective on the case. Captain Medvil knows all of this as well as anyone else.

"I didn't want to drive all the way up there," I say, "in case I had to be back here on another job. Besides, you know as well as I do that they're going to be processing the scene for a while and that's even before it all gets to the lab. I have some time. I thought I'd be of use here."

"You really can't relax, can you?" he asks. "I mean, don't you have any hobbies?"

I think back to the hobby that I was just about to start: writing books about the fictionalized cases that I have been working on.

Is that really a hobby if in your downtime, you do exactly the same thing that you do for your work?

"Listen, it's just ... all I can do is work, okay? Otherwise, my mind just goes nuts. I get listless. I can't just sit around and do nothing. Since this call came in, I thought that I could go and help them find this guy."

"Okay, well, I'm doing this as a favor to you. Okay? Don't forget that. I will need you to return sometime. I'm going to call you on it."

"I understand, Captain." I nod.

"Go and take this case. Hopefully it'll be a quick one. There's a body in the apartment."

"Who called it in?"

"The father of the guy who's renting the place."

"I got it."

"If you feel like you're not up to it, you can get off this case anytime," Captain Medvil says. "Suddenly I'm sounding more like a father than a boss. I know that you've been through a lot and I don't want to make things more difficult for you."

"It's going to be fine. Work is going to do me some good," I say and walk away from him feeling the burn of his gaze in the back of my neck.

I ARRIVE at a two-story apartment building with low ceilings and thick concrete patios out front. It's an older building with a style that was popular in the 70s.

I've lived in a building kind of like this one and due to the wideness and the thickness of the concrete patio resulted with very little lighting coming in on the inside.

I head upstairs through the open lobby door to the second floor. Each apartment door goes straight outside and there's a small, walkable garden in the center of the building exposed to the sky. This kind of structure can only exist in California or the Southwest that gets very little rain.

On the second landing, I can see the flashing lights below. The police cars are right outside with just the lights on, not the sound. There are deputies sectioning off the scene, preventing people from going up and down the stairs to the apartment.

Questioning the neighbors, Deputy Olson, who had just recently had his thirtieth birthday party at the department introduces me to a devastated man in his early sixties named Peter Millian.

"You are the father of Nicholas Millian?" I ask. "He rents this apartment?"

"Yes," Peter says, shaking his head.

"He was the one who found the girl," Deputy Olson whispers into my ear.

I excuse myself for a moment to take a look at the scene and tell Olson to keep him here. I walk past the crime scene technicians who give me a pair of booties to put on so that I don't contaminate anything in the bedroom.

The door is open and the lights are on. A small woman's body is lying behind the bed next to the curtains. The curtains are the kind that pool at the bottom, too long for the wall, and she lies on top with her face buried in them.

Given the trail of blood, she probably rolled off the bed. Dressed in jeans and a tank top with a flannel shirt on top, the dead woman has her hair pulled up into a ponytail. Part of her head is covered in blood from where she was shot in the temple.

I won't know much about how she was killed or even her name until the scene is properly processed. I walk back out, take off my booties, and pull Peter Millian aside.

"Can you please tell me everything that happened here, Mr. Millian?" I ask.

He's dressed in a t-shirt even though it's cold outside. He looks like he works out and takes care of himself. His hair is peppered with gray and he has a nice olive tan to his skin, like he has just gotten back from a tanning salon or a trip to the tropics.

"I haven't talked to my son for a while," he says.

"How long was that, Mr. Millian?"

"Peter, please." He looks up at me, but he doesn't look into my eyes. He looks somewhere past me.

"When you say that you haven't talked to him for a while, how long was that?"

"Just a couple of days. He wasn't answering his phone, so I decided to drive up here and see where he is."

"Where do you live?"

"Down in Long Beach, so not really far. I should've come up here earlier."

"Can you tell me a little bit about your son Nick?"

"Oh, he's such a great kid," Peter says, beaming proudly. "He just came back from active duty. He has all these plans. He is going to West Los Angeles College."

"Oh, yeah? Just started?" I ask.

"Yeah, this semester. Is taking anthropology, calculus, and another class, I can't remember. Yeah, just trying to get his basic coursework out of the way, so he can transfer to a four-year school."

"Oh, wow."

"Yeah, he wants to go to University of Southern California."

"USC?"

"Yeah, I know. It's expensive and really hard to get into, but he really thinks he can do it."

"What are his plans after that? What does he want to do for a living?"

"He isn't sure. He is all over the place. He's kind of an older student now, twenty-six years old."

"Do you happen to know who that girl is in his apartment?" I ask, steering the conversation back to the crime scene.

Peter shakes his head and looks away from me. I know that her purse and wallet is there along with her phone, so it probably won't be too hard to identify her, but I also want to know how much Peter knows about his son.

Peter shakes his head and says that he's not sure, his son doesn't have a girlfriend.

"Does he see many girls romantically?" I ask. "Or boys?"

"He's straight," Peter says without missing a beat. "But I haven't heard him talk about too many girlfriends. He's kind of a loner. He likes to play his guitar and he has a few close friends, but that's pretty much it. He likes to play a lot of video games."

"Got it," I say.

"I know that word loner probably means something very bad in your line of work." Peter leans closer to me.

He puts his hand on my arm and it feels uncomfortable.

He's trying to convince me of something, make me believe something that he does.

"I know that my son didn't do this. He's a wonderful sweet boy and I have no idea how that girl ended up in his apartment, dead no less, but my son didn't do this."

"Will you be able to help us find him?" I ask. "Just to get to the bottom of all of this?"

"Of course. Of course I will," he says.

I walk away from him a little bit perplexed. I know that Peter Millian believes that his son didn't kill that girl, but women don't just show up in men's apartments without them having some connection to them.

Officer Olson walks up to me and asks me what I think. He's the kind of person who looks like he never misses a session at the gym: bulging biceps, a snugly fit uniform, and very earnest expression on his face.

You'd think that he is a flirt, but he's not.

He's engaged to be married to his high school girlfriend and they've been together for years. Unlike many others in this department, he's not just pretending to be faithful, he actually is.

He's one of those guys who's a little bit too honest, shoots straight, and isn't a player.

"What do you think is going on here, Detective?" he asks.

We walk around the corner to make sure that Peter Millian can't hear us.

"I'm afraid that it's probably a domestic violence incident."

He nods.

"They were probably romantically linked. I don't know, maybe boyfriend and girlfriend or a little more casual. His dad didn't seem to know much about it."

He nods.

"I hate to say this, but he's a Marine and we all know that they struggle with Post-Traumatic Stress Disorder," I mumble, pacing back and forth. "A lot of them can be quite violent with their significant others and maybe that's the case here. We won't know anything for sure until we find him. I'm leaning toward, they go into a fight, he shot her, and then fled. But we can't make any assumptions."

Officer Olson nods his head again in agreement.

"Will you put out an all-points bulletin on him and his car? I think he drives a Toyota Camry, but double check with the father about the license plate and all of the details. This just happened. I'm not sure how long she's been there, but he probably didn't get out of the state yet or maybe even the county. I wonder if he's just driving around LA thinking of a way to get out of this mess."

"I would be," Olson says and I give him a little smile.

"I'm just sorry that his father has to deal with this," I say. "He really thinks he's a good guy."

3

_____

After processing the body that was found in Nicholas Millian's apartment, it falls on me to notify next of kin about her untimely death. This is a part of the job that I hate the most.

The girl is twenty-one years old and her name is Janine Sato. From the picture on her driver's license, she looks to be of Japanese descent and I find her mom's phone number on her phone that was also at the apartment.

I arrive at Mrs. Sato's apartment in Koreatown later that evening and she answers the door wearing nothing but a bathrobe.

She's a small, frail woman with her hair in curlers and as soon as she sees my face and I tell her who I am, she begins to sob.

It's never good to have the police show up on your doorstep in the middle of the night, but I have the worst news possible: her only daughter has been murdered.

She speaks English without even a slight accent. It sounds like she grew up in California.

There are framed pictures of Janine all over the living room and the console table as well additional ones hanging all over the walls. She has two brothers, both older, both married.

Through her sobs, Mrs. Sato tells me that her husband had passed away just last year from a sudden heart attack. After she calms down a bit and makes herself a cup of tea, we sit down on the couch and I ask her to tell me about Janine.

"She was always such a vibrant child, fun, and outgoing. She loved to dance. She had many different groups of friends, all throughout high school."

"College?" I ask.

"She went to West Los Angeles College to save some money and her dream was to go to USC."

That's exactly where Peter Millian said his son wanted to go.

"Was Janine seeing anybody," I ask, "romantically?"

"No, not that I know of. She had a boyfriend from high school for a while, but then things didn't work out."

"Would you know if she was seeing someone?"

"What do you mean?" she asks, pulling her bathrobe tight to her neck.

DRESSED IN PINK SLIPPERS, which are a perfect match to her turban, suddenly I become keenly aware of the fact that I'm still wearing my boots even though there is a collection of shoes by the door.

"Well, please don't take this the wrong way, but your daughter was living at home. What was her dating life like? Did she bring guys back home here or did she spend the night at their place? Did she stay with girlfriends?"

"She pretty much came and went as she pleased. I didn't have a curfew or anything like that if that's what you're implying."

I nod.

"She has a few close friends, but my daughter is twenty-one. I'm very well aware of the fact that kids that age have sex and as long as she was using protection and being safe, I had no problem with that."

"Did your daughter ever happen to mention the name *Nick Millian*?"

"Yes, he was her friend."

"What did she tell you?"

"They did theater together. They painted decorations for the plays."

"Oh, really?" I ask. "Were they ever romantically involved?"

"I thought that he was a nice kid. He came over a few times for dinner. They seemed to get along really well, but when I asked her about dating him, she said that they weren't good for each other. She said they were just friends."

"Oh, okay." I look down at my notepad, keeping my face stoic. "Do you think that he was more into her than she was into him?"

"I don't know. He seemed friendly and they laughed a lot. We played a few board games after dinner, but I didn't get the sense that he was into her that way. Actually, I thought he might be gay."

"Oh, really?"

"Well, I didn't want to say anything because he wasn't talking about it publicly, so it's not really any of my business. I thought that maybe he is and I was going to ask Janine about it. That's probably why they weren't together."

"Huh." I nod to myself, uncertain as to where to go from here.

I was so convinced that he was a guy that she said no to and that's why he might've hurt her.

Now this reminds me why it's so important to keep an open mind, I say to myself.

You can't ever close yourself off to possibilities just because the case looks like it's something, doesn't mean that it is.

I wonder if his father knows and write a note to myself to ask him.

After getting all the possible information I can from Mrs. Sato, I leave her alone in her grief.

Giving her my card, I promise to be in touch as soon as I know anything. Tomorrow, Mrs. Sato will have to go to the medical examiner's office and do an official identification of Janine's body.

I know that she'll spend all night praying that we are wrong.

I'm also certain that seeing her daughter tomorrow will cause her more pain than she has ever felt in her whole life and yet there's nothing I can do about it except find the guy who did that to her.

I GET HOME exhausted and worn out, but in the way where I'm emotionally tired rather than physically. I grab my running shoes and change into a pair of my least favorite leggings with a sports bra, pulling a sweatshirt over my head.

I don't go on runs often or rather I'm trying to get better at it. I'm not much into exercise, and I tend to binge on food which isn't doing me any favors.

With all of these hours that I put in at work, I need to get some of my energy out in whatever way possible.

The sun is just starting to set and I head west toward the ocean. I'm too far away from Santa Monica, but I love this time of the day.

It's warm and comforting. With the sun just hovering over the horizon, the chill is going to take over in a little bit, but not yet.

We all know it's coming, but it's not here now. I lift my legs slowly at first, but after a few blocks, I pick up the pace.

When I get a stitch in my side, I slow down again and jog at a comfortable pace.

I check my watch and when I get to two miles, I celebrate by taking a little bit of a break.

My time is horrendous. I used to run this distance five minutes faster back in college, but given the fact that I haven't exercised consistently in ages, I'm proud of myself for doing anything at all.

My thoughts drift back to Luke and everything that has happened between us. It was supposed to be just a casual relationship, if I can even call it that: nothing serious, just having a little fun.

I had already sworn off dating anyone in law enforcement after my breakup with Thomas and everything that has happened as a result.

When I met Luke, I had no expectations. In fact, I promised myself that I wouldn't even go out with him. Naturally, that was one of a number of promises that were broken.

Luke is a bit of an enigma.

He's kind and sweet, but also a little bit harsh around the edges. He isn't afraid to challenge me and to tell me the truth. I like that more than I will admit.

The last time that I seen him, we snuck around. Even though that made it even hotter, the fire and the burn between us was impossible to forget.

Now I wonder if maybe it was the fact that we were sneaking around. He isn't married or in a relationship.

I hate men who cheat on their wives and girlfriends. I'm not either. I would never date someone like that.

You should be able to be honest with who you are and what you want. I'm not interested in people who thrive on dishonesty, but when it came to sneaking around, yes, we did do that.

The problem is that Violet is my sister and she's a missing person. Luke is one of the FBI agents assigned to her case.

Being romantically linked to me is a big no-no. The thing is that we weren't in any official relationship when she went missing and when he got sent to Big Bear to work both on her case and Natalie D'Achille's disappearance.

My thoughts return to the way we handled our last interaction together. It wasn't my finest hour.

I was angry and upset. We had just spent some time alone in a hotel room and had the most mind-blowing afternoon.

Then just as I was about to go back to LA to handle a case for work, he told me that he was going on a date. Apparently, he had been set up by his cousin way before we met.

That all was true, except I got upset. I got mad at him.

I told him that he can go on a date with whoever he wants and we had a fight. I said things I didn't mean and then I didn't apologize.

After that, it got worse. We didn't talk. I know that he went on that date. I don't know what happened, but then an ex-boyfriend of mine from college asked me to meet up.

I haven't seen him in years and I ran into him going on a run just like this. I told him yes.

I don't know what I would have said if Luke and I were actually together, but now I wonder.

Nothing happened with Mark. Of course, he wanted something to happen, but I stopped it.

Now everything that was so right with Luke, seems off somehow.

Wrong.

Off-kilter.

I walk most of the way back, half limping from the stitch in my side. The music blasting in my earphones is no longer enough to take my thoughts away from where they have drifted.

This is why I work so much. This is why I don't like to be alone with my thoughts.

It's easier to just be somewhere else.

It's easier to think about something than my own problems.

I get back to my apartment building, gasping for air. I ran the last half a mile, pushing myself hard through the pain.

My lungs are screaming and yet, no matter how many breaths I take, none are enough.

A loud motorcycle roars by me, deafening me.

Hasn't he ever heard of a muffler? I say silently to myself, annoyed with the noise that I have to put up with living in the city.

You'd think that after all of these years I'd be used to it, but I'm not. There was a time when I craved all of this.

I moved to New York and then to Los Angeles. I couldn't be more excited to get away from the cramped, small town where I grew up.

It all felt so stifling and claustrophobic.

Everyone knew your business no matter how much you tried to keep it to yourself. If I ever did anything wrong, I was certain that all my mom's friends at the school would tell her.

For many years, my mom worked as a librarian at the Big Bear High School. She wasn't a teacher, thank God, but she was there and she knew exactly what was going on. Worse yet, she knew every one of my teachers.

They were friends. They went to potlucks. They went to their kids' birthday parties.

So, when I was getting out of line, when I spent most of my days lying, sneaking out, and hanging out with people I wasn't supposed to, she heard all about it.

My mom still works at the high school. Only part time now.

The library position was downsized. It's not like a high school needs a librarian, right? She has picked up a few shifts at the public library in town, minimum wage work, no benefits.

This isn't a big city library. She could probably make more waiting tables, but that's not what she has her Master's in. She's the type of person that likes to correct people's spelling, emails, and text messages. She acts like she doesn't mind the low salary, but I know that it gets to her.

I climb up the stairs to my apartment. I notice that I need to ask my landlord to paint my front door.

The green paint is chipping on the side, making it look rather shabby and not at all chic. I put my key in the door and as soon as I open it, I see *her* sitting on the couch, sobbing.

4

Sydney Sutka and I have been friends for a few years.

She has a graduate degree in psychology and she hasn't taken the most conventional route to become a police officer. So, we connected immediately.

Her thick, dark hair rolls in waves with each sob. I rush over to her and put my arm around her, hugging her tightly.

I ask her what's wrong over and over again, but every time she comes up for air to say something, she loses it and gets choked up.

I pat her back, trying to calm her down.

"I think he's cheating on me," Sydney says through the sobs.

This takes me by surprise.

Patrick Flannery, her fiancé, is about as salt of the earth as one gets. He's an FBI agent from a nice family, with three or four siblings. His parents have been married for years and all of his siblings are, too.

When the two of them got together, I figured that would be it for her. They'd be happily together for years to come and I'd be their sad little friend who could never find the right guy to date.

"What makes you say that?" I ask. "Why do you think he's cheating on you?"

She shakes her head trying to get it out, but she still needs more time. After a few more gulps of air, she finally looks up at me with her big almond eyes, wiping the mascara under her lids with the back of her hand.

"I found the secret folder on his phone," she whispers. "He gave me the password and he wanted me to text someone back when he was driving. Then when he was taking a shower the other day, his phone was there and I had the password so I just looked. It was a joke at first. I was just curious. I didn't expect to find anything."

I nod and rub the small of her back.

"I had no idea that I was going to find something. I had no idea that... God, I'm such an idiot."

She takes her head and begins to cry again.

I ask her for more details.

She explains that apparently she found a folder with pictures, explicit ones of different girls from different sites.

I ask her if maybe they are just pictures of porn stars: no one specifically, no one important.

"No, I thought that, too, but I kept looking and saw pictures of him *with them* in a hot tub," she says, pulling out her phone. "I just can't believe that I was so stupid. I sent a bunch of them to myself. Look!"

We start to go through them.

In the first one, Patrick has blurry eyes, clearly intoxicated, sitting in an enormous jacuzzi with two girls kissing each other and him.

There are a few other guys there as well and it looks like Vegas in the background.

There's a video of him playing pool and slapping the girl's butt while they both grind against each other.

There's video of him, naked, drinking champagne off of her naked breasts.

"When was he doing all of this?" I ask.

"I don't know. He said he was working a lot more than he was. I'm just such an idiot."

"Listen, you know he's an FBI agent. He's good at lying."

"I should have known. I'm a cop," Sydney says. "I was going to marry this guy. I was going to have kids with him. I mean, I thought that I actually found a decent person."

"I'm really sorry, honey. What happened when you found all of this?"

She shakes her head.

"Did you talk to him?"

"No."

"You didn't?"

"No. I just left. I couldn't handle it. I didn't want to have a fight. I had to go to work. I don't know. I just was so dumb. I guess I should have confronted him, but I needed to figure out my feelings first. I just can't believe that I was going to marry this person. Like, who is he?"

Sydney looks down at her one-carat princess cut diamond ring and pulls it off her finger.

When she throws it across the room, it hits the window on the other end. I want to tell her that she's overreacting and that she needs to give Patrick a chance to explain, but I don't want to. I don't think she is doing anything that I wouldn't.

"Can I stay here tonight?" She sobs and takes off her boots.

"Yes, of course." I nod.

I head to my closet and give her a pair of the comfiest pajamas that I own. She changes right in the living room, and I turn away and go to the kitchen to pour us some wine.

I change as well and give her my robe. After we're both wearing the comfiest clothes we possibly can, all wrapped up in a cloud, with a glass of wine in our hands, she turns to me and tells me that she's sorry.

"For what? You have nothing to be sorry for."

She shakes her head and I wait for her to explain.

"I lied to you. I mean, not overtly, but I was such an idiot."

"What do you mean?" I ask, taking another sip.

The Chardonnay puts me at ease and I'm certain that whatever she's apologizing for hardly matters.

"When you found out that Thomas was cheating, I judged you. I thought to myself, there's no way that you couldn't know. I mean, you're dating someone, you're with him a lot. You have to know something, right?"

I hate the fact that she's bringing up Thomas. I still feel raw about talking about him.

Thomas is a cop who works in my department. He's someone I see on an almost daily basis. We dated for a while and I thought that we were going to be together forever. I never thought that way about anyone before.

In fact, reflecting back on that moment, I feel like a fool.

He made me laugh. We liked the same things. We hated the same things. We seemed to have a lot in common.

He asked me to marry him in a French restaurant and when he got down on one knee, everyone clapped and we got free dessert.

Then I found out the truth. He cheated on me and is having a baby with someone else.

From what I heard from the rumor mill at work is that she's a court reporter and he started seeing her about six months ago. At first it was casual and they were going to break things off, but then she got pregnant.

I guess they're together. The problem is *not* that he didn't want to be with me. The problem is that he led me on and didn't even bother to tell me the truth.

"When that happened to you," Sydney says, reaching over and taking my hand in hers, "I felt so bad for you. I was so embarrassed and just horrified, but I said to myself that could never happen to me. I would know that he's a cheater."

I shake my head and look away. It's too hard to look directly at her.

"You know what? You couldn't have known and I couldn't have known. I'm just really sorry that I was such a bad friend."

"You were not a bad friend." I squeeze her hand back. "We all think things like that sometimes and what's important is that you were there for me when I needed you. I did need you then and I'll be there for you through this."

"I just feel like such an idiot, you know?" She wipes more tears.

I nod.

"I mean, you told me not to date people in law enforcement and obviously we all know that because then you end up working with them, but with Patrick, it was different. You know, things clicked and his family was so nice and everyone is so happily married."

"Well, as far as you know," I joke.

She raises her eyebrows and opens her mouth to say something, but the words don't quite come out.

"Listen, we all want to know the truth about everyone that we're with and we think we do. Given the fact that we're detectives, we put additional stress on our ability to figure people out, but it's not that easy when your heart is involved. You couldn't have known anything about Patrick."

"I could have if I looked in his phone earlier," she insists.

"Yeah, but then you wouldn't have trusted him and what kind of relationship starts out with no trust?" I say, taking a sip of my wine. "No, you have to give it a chance. In the future, you'll have to give it a chance as well. You'll have to accept that the next guy is telling you the truth. Otherwise you won't be able to move on, you know?"

"Is that what you're doing with Luke?" she asks.

I bite the inside of my cheek.

I wish I could tell her the truth. I wish I could admit that's precisely what I'm doing.

I'm just giving it a shot and I'm jumping in with both feet, but I have my doubts. I got upset with him for no reason at all.

My past and the fact that I've been hurt is all there. It's all coming to the surface at the worst possible time.

"I'm trying, you know?" I finally say. "You'll have to try, too, but not tonight. Tonight you just have to lick your wounds and try to figure out what you want to do."

5

_____

S ydney sleeps over in my living room after I make up the couch and we both wake up right before six the following morning. Before I get ready for work, normally I like to sleep in if I can, but today's not one of those days.

The sooner that I can get all of this taken care of, the sooner I can get back to trying to figure out what happened to Violet.

I have a few bagels in the pantry, along with jam and some vegan cream cheese.

"How's that going not eating dairy and meat?" she asks, spreading the cheese on her freshly toasted bagel.

"It's okay."

"Don't you miss it? Bacon, eggs?"

"I still have eggs," I admit. "I'm kind of trying to take it slow. I have dairy on occasion when I'm out, but I don't buy any to have at home. Easing into it, so to say."

"What about the meat?"

"Been having vegetarian burgers and some of that imitation meat, but no, I can't say I really miss it. I've been trying to eat more vegetables anyway, as well as beans and lentils."

"Well, you're a better person than I am." Sydney smiles, taking a big bite of her bagel and wiping the corners of her mouth.

"You know, you can do it, too, if you want to."

"Yeah, I think I may, but not quite yet. I'm too stressed out by everything, if you know what I mean?"

"You have to do it at a good time in your life." I nod.

"It's like making any other change. Speaking of that, how's the workout regimen?"

"Start and stop. I ran last night, but I didn't for a few previous days."

"Well, now that you're traveling so much between here and back home, I'm sure it's hard."

I wish that I could say that's entirely what's going on, but in reality, I'm just not really into it.

I'm hesitant to bring up Patrick, but I also feel awkward not saying anything, given the fact that the whole reason why she slept over is because of what happened.

"So, what are your thoughts about…you know?" I ask, trying to be as casual as possible.

"I don't know. I have to figure out a way to get my stuff out of that apartment."

She shoves a quarter of the bagel into her mouth, chewing fervently.

"Are you going to talk to him?"

"I was going to. But now I don't know. I keep going back and forth."

"What do you mean?" I ask. "Don't you want to just lay into him and have a big fight?"

"No, I don't."

I nod.

"I'm just exhausted. I'm angry and I mainly don't want to hear more lies. If he hadn't told me about it, I think he'll just make up some stuff. Tell me I'm wrong. I'm just over it. What can he really tell me? What can he really say? They are pictures of him and videos of him with all of these women. I mean, why did he do this?"

"I don't know." I shrug.

"Because he wanted to. He thought he could get away with it."

"I'm really sorry, Syd," I say, wrapping my hand around her shoulders. She just shrugs me off.

"Listen. Maybe I can change my mind about everything."

"You mean to go back to him?" I gasp.

"No, no, not that, but relationships are complicated. If I see him, I may yell at him, start a bonfire, burn his clothes. Now, that's an idea! Will you help me go to our apartment and get some of my stuff?"

"Yes, of course," I say.

"Also, can I stay with you?" she asks.

"Of course. You don't even have to ask."

"Thanks. That's such a relief. That's the problem when you live with someone. You kind of have nowhere to go."

"You can stay with me as long as you want," I say. I give her another hug and this time she holds on.

I drive over to her apartment in my car. She drives hers and I help her load a bunch of things into my trunk and back seat.

She packs garbage bags full of her clothes and grabs a few fixtures and decor items from the mantel and the dining room table.

She also packs a box full of books from the bottom shelves of the bookcase, making the apartment look about as cleared out as you can with two cars of things.

We drive back over to my place and I quickly regret my decision in letting her not just stay, but move in.

When she asked, I thought that she would grab a suitcase or two and live out of those until she found her own place, not actually pack up all of her stuff and move in.

It takes about four trips up and down the stairs to unload all of her stuff. I'm completely spent and it's not even eight in the morning.

"God, I need a nap," I say, sitting down on my couch for a moment and looking around with all of her things stacked in ugly piles in my living room.

"I'm really sorry about all of this," Sydney says, looking around as well and biting her lower lip. "I didn't realize that I took so much stuff."

I shrug. What else is there to say in this situation?

"I can go back."

"No, of course not, that's ridiculous. We'll figure it out. You can put some stuff in my room or when you find a new place, whatever."

I'm not particularly picky about my decorations and I'm not someone who uses catalogs to design my living space, but all of this clutter in boxes and bags gives me a bit of anxiety. I want to get out of this place as soon as I can.

Luckily, my phone rings. I don't recognize the number at first, but as soon as I answer, I know exactly who it is. His voice is frantic and out of control, just like it was yesterday.

It's Peter Millian, the father of the Marine in whose apartment we found the dead girl.

"He's using his credit cards," Peter says in a rushed, frantic way. "Detective Carr, did you hear me?"

"Yes, yes, I'm here. Who? Who's using the credit cards?"

"My son or maybe someone else using his credit cards?" he asks as if that thought just occurred to him. "I don't know, but I've been tracking them on my banking app and he's withdrawn $400 at three different ATMs about thirty minutes apart, just this morning."

"Okay, okay, that's good. Thanks for letting me know. Why don't you come into the precinct to show me what you found and we can contact the bank to get the footage, to see if it is your son."

"I'll be there as soon as I can," he says and hangs up.

"What's wrong?" Sydney asks as I turn the mood ring around my finger in circles. I fill her in.

"That's good, right? Maybe it's his son using the ATM."

"Yeah, it probably is. The problem is that I kind of feel bad for him," I admit. "He's being very helpful and you know how this goes. It doesn't look good. His son probably killed her and maybe had some sort of psychotic break or whatever. His father is so certain that he didn't do it, couldn't have done it, and he's doing all of these things to give us the evidence against his son. I'm grateful, as a detective, but my heart goes out to him as a fellow human being."

"You really don't think that his son could be innocent?"

"A girl was found in his apartment," I say. "His friend was shot and he's gone. If he's innocent, why isn't he here?"

———

PETER COMES to the precinct less than an hour later. He must have drove like hell to get here, probably breaking as many speed limits on the way as he could.

He shows me his computer and the bank withdrawals.

It will take some time for the footage to actually be sent over, but after making a call to the security personnel at the bank, I'm welcome to come look at it right now.

I usually don't like to do this, but I decide to take Peter along with me just to speed things along. I'll be able to know if he recognizes his son and that will give us a good starting point to figure out if he was indeed in the area making the withdrawals.

The first bank moves swiftly.

The guard quickly shows us to the back office and pulls up the footage from the ATM. I have memorized what Nick looks like from a photo that Peter had shown me: beefy with thick jowls and a crew cut popular with the Marines, not entirely dissimilar from what my fellow police officers like to do with their hair.

Much to my surprise, the guy I see in the ATM recording is anything but that.

He's tall, skinny, and lanky. He's wearing a hat, but the camera angle points up rather than down, directly at his face.

He hardly looks a day over eighteen years old and probably weighs no more than a hundred and ten pounds, soaking wet.

"No, no, no, no," Peter says, pointing at the screen. "That's not him, that's *not* my son."

"That's the guy who used his card," the security guard says with a casual shrug, completely unbothered.

We watch the footage again and again, then make our way to the next ATM right outside a 7-Eleven.

It takes longer to retrieve this footage, and it requires us to wait around for some time for the guard to show up to access the recordings. In the meantime, I consume about two bags of pretzels.

"No, absolutely not!" Peter shakes his head, getting animated.

I lean closer and confirm that it's the same guy who did the other withdrawal; only this time he's wearing sunglasses. The features of his face are very distinct: pointy nose, pointy cheekbones, and pointy chin. It's clearly him, but *who* is he?

"One possible explanation is that your son lost his card or threw it away and this kid picked it up and used it," I say.

"How would he know the pin code?" Peter asks.

"They'd have to be friends. He'd have to tell him."

"No, my son would never say that," Peter insists, shuffling his feet as he walks back and forth. "Ever since he was a teenager, he always kept that pin code close to his heart."

"He would never share it with anyone?"

"No. Besides, he had a lot of money in that bank account."

"What do you mean?" I ask. "Like savings?"

He nods.

"How much?" I ask. "Peter. You have to tell me. This is all relevant."

"He had $58,000 saved up from all three tours in the Middle East. I mean, he spent some of his money, yes, went to Vegas, partied a little, but that's what he had left the last time he told me."

"What was he going to do?"

"He didn't know yet. Maybe USC or maybe buy a house, but he was saving it. He was a good boy. Since it's his bank card, there's no way he would've given his pin code to any friend, let alone *this* punk."

I nod.

We go to the last location, a small ATM attached to a wall wedged between a pizza shop and a hair salon.

We call the number on the screen and the people on the other end say that it's going to be a little bit before anyone can get back to us. I leave my number and stress the urgency of the situation.

Back at the precinct, I try to figure out what to do. I send Peter home despite the fact that he keeps insisting on sticking around and figuring this out with me.

I wonder if he thinks that I'm incompetent because I'm young or a woman. Maybe both.

On the other hand, he might just be a sad father desperate to find his son. The only thing I can do is promise him that I'll do my best and get to the bottom of this as quickly as possible.

I update Captain Medvil on what I've found so far and I quickly print out the pictures from the ATM footage to distribute to the patrol cops making the rounds in the area.

They're going to canvas the businesses and ask questions to find out the name of this kid.

If we're lucky, he doesn't live too far away and someone knows who he is. If we're unlucky, he's a stranger just passing through, which will make everything a lot more complicated.

6

It's hard to explain exactly how defeated I feel as I drive back to my home. My sister is not there and the darkness that descends seems to be scarier and more devoid of life with every passing moment.

After my father's death, I never wanted to go back there, but my mom had the opposite reaction.

She never wanted to leave.

She cleaned up their bedroom and tried to make it look like all the blood, the guts, and everything horrendous that had happened there didn't. I wonder how other people who have lost loved ones and have seen the grotesqueness of the scenes feel about them.

The world is a dark place and when I became a detective, I wanted to right so many wrongs. As the years drag on, I realize why drinking is such a problem in my profession.

You can't make everything right. Even if you do get justice, even if you do find out who did it, the truth is all you have.

You don't get that person back.

To this day, my mother insists that what happened to my father was suicide. She thinks that he took his own life, but I know different.

Okay, not know for sure, but I think differently. My father was a drug dealer and a drug runner. I never found out the depths of everything that he was involved with. My mother hid it from me. She never talked about it. Now, I wonder why not.

I used to think it's because she closed her eyes to that part of him, that secret life. All of that darkness that he unleashed onto the world.

I can't help but wonder what happened to all of that money, the extent of what he did or how far he got up the chain of command.

Was there even a chain of command?

There had to be.

He wasn't just a low-level thug.

If he were, then he would have gotten caught much sooner.

But I don't think that his death has anything to do with my sister's, if that's where you think this is going.

I let my mind wander as I drive up the narrow mountain road.

Even though the FBI is now involved in searching for her, the days keep passing and you don't have to be in law enforcement to know that her case is going to go cold soon.

They don't have much.

They don't have a body.

They don't have any forensic evidence.

They just have a bag of clothes that she wore and that's it.

Did she change? Did someone make her change? Why?

The days are short and the nights are long. During this part of the year, snow has been cleared up and pushed along the sides of the road. It's dirty and black now, missing all of the romance of a snowy mountain day.

There was a time in my life that I wanted to get a cabin in the woods on some acreage away from everyone else. I'm not a very social person. I'll go out to bars. I'll hang out with Sydney, but I can count my friends on a few fingers.

I'm more social online. It's easier that way. You don't have to respond in real time. You can do it when you have a moment, when you're feeling bored, or when you have some time to kill.

This is probably the way it always is or was for introverts. Hanging out with people exhausts us. Our energy gets drained and then we need that alone time to get it all back.

When I was growing up, being an introvert was called being shy. The last thing that someone who is introverted ever wants to hear is someone calling them shy in front of strangers. It's an announcement to the world that there's something wrong with you and that you're not like everyone else.

I don't want to give you the impression that I had a difficult childhood. Most of the time, I didn't.

Most of my memories are happy ones: playing in the backyard, going swimming in the lake, and skiing.

It was always in nature where I found myself to be the happiest. It was always in nature when the world seemed to make a little bit more sense.

Before driving all the way over to my mom's house, I pull over right in front of the big boulders on one side of the lake, get out, and go on a little walk.

Nature has always brought me peace. It has always put me at ease when nothing else could.

Working this job has taken me away from all that.

I work in the city and I deal with city problems. I'm always in my car and most of the time, that's not enough.

The pines surround me, long brooding ones that cast wide shadows all around. I climb up one of the boulders and just moving my legs in that way that isn't just walking on asphalt fills me with glee.

This is where I used to hang out a lot as a kid.

My dad would bring me here when I was five or six years old. We would climb these boulders and we wouldn't care that the people that own the houses right around here, the mega-mansions, would complain. Most of them were hardly ever home and that was just fine by us.

I was eighteen years old when Violet was born and the father and mother that she grew up with were drastically different from the ones that I had.

On one hand, they were more mature, but on the other, they were also more selfish. Sometimes you give your firstborn too much attention and other times you try to make up for all the mistakes that you made with your first one when you have your second.

That's what it was like for Violet. Sometimes she was allowed to do things that I wasn't and other times her life was so much more magical than my own.

Unfortunately, she never knew our dad, not really. He died when she was a toddler.

I wonder what kind of father he would be the second time around. I wonder what things he would have made up for and what he would have done better.

I sometimes think what kind of mother I would be had I become one when I was in my early twenties and what kind of mother I would be when I become one in my thirties.

I wasn't pregnant long and there was nothing I could do about the miscarriage, but in that span of a few weeks, when I was still in college, my whole life turned upside down.

Suddenly, I started living for the person I was going to be, as the mom who was going to be taking care of this baby. Nine months didn't seem like enough time to prepare, not at all, but that's all I had or so I thought.

It turned out that I had so much less. No one knows about my miscarriage. Maybe one day, if I'm ever close enough to someone to get married, I'll let them know. I'll share that part of me that is filled with secrets, but the problem is that I have so many other secrets as well.

The boulder that I sit on top of is smooth but hard to the touch. I dig my sneakers into it, but that's hardly necessary as there's so much friction already.

I breathe in and out slowly and deliberately. I need to go back to find out anything more that I can about my missing sister and to help my mom, but I can't bring myself to move.

Violet was always someone who laughed very easily and she cried easily, too. It was like she had this precipice of emotions. Sometimes she was angry, sometimes she was sad, and sometimes she was happy. Sometimes she was all of those things, all at once. I know that's what drove Mom nuts.

Mom is a librarian who likes rules and order. She organized my childhood books according to the Dewey Decimal System and she even made a small little card catalog of our home library.

In addition to working with books at work, she also had a big collection in our house. There was a whole separate bedroom devoted just to books.

When I saw *Beauty and the Beast* for the first time, I recognized myself in Belle, beautiful yet quiet and reserved, being held hostage by some mysterious stranger in a castle full of books.

Well, that was kind of a fantasy come true, especially for a twelve-year-old girl with an imagination that was a little too big for her britches.

I adjust my seat on the rocks just as one side of my butt cheek falls asleep. It's cool against my body, which feels nice.

7

I was an only child for so long that I've often felt like an only child, even after my sister came into existence.

Of course, I never forgot about her, nothing like that. It's more that she appeared when I was already a grownup. So, when I thought about my childhood, it was just me.

I don't want to give you the impression that I was lonely. I was anything but that.

My parents were very involved, always going to my events and always encouraging me to participate in things, even though I didn't really want to.

My mom was even more like that with Violet. She loved to write and take pictures and make videos, so she wanted her to participate in the newspaper and the photography club.

Violet did join last year, but what about this one? I can't quite remember now. It seems like parts of her are vanishing already.

When I was younger, I thought of her as my baby. There were already girls that I knew who had children and she was a baby that I spent a lot of time with, especially that first summer when she was born.

I came home to help take care of her and the days were filled with a lot of laughter, swinging, and naps. Being a mother is hard, probably at any age and I've never been one full-time, but that summer I really loved it. I loved mothering her. My mom worked full-time and took on extra shifts since Dad's money either came in buckets or not at all.

My father was a drug dealer, but for many years he didn't provide much. I don't know the details of what happened, but money was hard to come by.

That's why I had so many loans when I graduated. That's why I'm still paying them off.

I climb down off the boulder and walk closer to the water. It moves slightly in the wind. It looks black now, illuminated by only a few lights somewhere in the distance.

I walk over to the public boat launch with a big gate out front that says that it's closed after dusk. I climb it and defy the rules, just like I did when I was a teenager.

When I was Violet's age, I had a friend who was so much more than a friend. We have known each other since we were in preschool.

His mom was an English teacher and she was good friends with my mom. We played a lot together. We were raised like we were brother and sister.

When we were twelve, something happened. I got feelings for him. I couldn't stop thinking about him. It was over the summer that we spent swimming in the lake and had taken his dad's boat out onto the water.

He was tan and muscular in that scrawny pre-teen way. He had poofy blonde hair and bright blue eyes and went by Nicky because he thought it made him sound cool.

He liked to draw on his arms using a ballpoint pen. They were thick elaborate designs to make it look like tattoos. I drew on my arms and legs, too, but my favorite was drawing on my white sneakers. I would color it all in and then go up to where the fabric was and doodle along there.

It drove our moms nuts. They vowed to never buy us new shoes again, but we would just laugh it off.

Nicky was a lot like Violet, quiet and reserved as strangers, but fun and outrageous with me and to those he knew well. The first time we kissed, we sat right here at the edge of this dock.

My left foot was in the water and my shoe sat on the dock next to me. We sat on the edge of this dock for a really long time, laughing, drinking Sprite, and eating green Jolly Ranchers until we were so high on sugar and our attraction to one another we could burst.

Just as the sun was setting, Nicky leaned over, closed his eyes, putting his hand on my arm to pull me close. He kissed me in a way that no one has ever kissed me before (or since). He was asking me permission, but he was also telling me what he wanted.

He was nervous and uncertain, and so was I. That was okay because we had each other. I knew right there and then that he would be the person that I would spend the rest of my life with.

It was a certainty and very much unlike the feeling I get when I meet men now as an adult. They are just dates, boyfriends, somebody to have a good time with for an evening or two or maybe a week, a month, a year. With Nicky, the world made sense. He got me. He understood everything there was about me.

At least that was what I thought back then and that's something that twelve year olds will probably think for as long as there are twelve year olds in the world.

That's what's great about being that age. You're no longer a child, but you're not a teenager either. You're in this strange existence between worlds; purgatory, some would call it.

I force myself up to my feet. I can't stay here much longer staring into this dark lake, remembering everything that I ran away from here for. I don't know if my hometown is just a bad place or is just a bad place *for me*, but I had no idea that my life would be filled with so much death and sadness until that afternoon when I lost Nicky.

We were on the boat, like we were for the millionth time that summer. It was a small boat with a small outward motor. We both were good swimmers and the lake was warm. We sunbathed for a while, listened to music, talked trash, and joked around with our friends that came by around noon.

Neither of us was drunk because we never had anything stronger than root beer aboard; that was one of his father's rules. It was a cardinal sin to drink on a boat and though we broke some rules, we always abided by that one.

I don't know exactly what happened *that* afternoon. My memories of that day are hazy and have only gotten hazier since. I thought that, at some point, memories would flood in, but they never did. I even went to have hypnosis and a few therapists to bring them out, all to no avail.

It was late in the afternoon and when the sun started to set, we knew we had to go back home. We had to go back to land. I remember I was talking about it while both of us were lying flat on our backs.

We hadn't talked about our kiss that happened only the day before. I was waiting for him to bring it up, but he never did and I never did. It was this big elephant in the room separating us.

The sun started to beat down hard. It gets into the nineties here in the summers, but with the thin air, it can feel even hotter, stronger, and more intense.

My eyelids started to feel heavy and I just let myself drift off. I knew that I'd probably wake up soon. I'd slept like that, taking little catnaps a thousand times before, but on that particular afternoon, it was a mistake.

When I finally opened my eyes, Nicky wasn't there.

The Hobbit by J. R. R. Tolkien, Nicky's favorite book, lay open flat with the highlighted pages and underlined sentences toward the fiberglass.

Still feeling woozy from opening my eyes, my heart jumped into my throat. I didn't know what to do.

I looked around everywhere, but the boat was barely fifteen feet long. There was literally nowhere to go.

There was a driver's seat, passenger seat, the front, and the back. That was it.

I looked around, I climbed out front, peering into the blue water. It was a little bit murky, it was a lake after all, and quite deep.

I didn't see anyone or anything. I had no idea *when* this could have happened or *where* he had gone.

What if another boat came by and he jumped in? I wondered.

Looking out into the distance, 360 degrees all around me, and there were no boats in sight.

Our friends had come and gone, but if someone had pulled up, the sound of the engine and their voices would have definitely woken me up. I knew that for sure.

I was asleep, but I wasn't deeply asleep. Besides, I was lying on the outside of the boat and it wasn't the most comfortable bed.

I picked up the intercom and called for help. I didn't know what to do.

I wanted to drive the boat back to dock, but I was afraid of leaving him.

While I waited for help to arrive, I jumped into the frigid water, put on my snorkeling mask, held my breath, and dove down over and over again, until I was spent and exhausted.

The visibility was less than a foot, but I plunged myself into the darkness just in case he was somewhere near.

The rest of what happened was even more of a blur.

The divers looked for his body for two days, eventually finding it about half a mile away from where we were.

There was an underground current that must have pulled him under and carried him away.

The officials had called it a *drowning*, but even now all of these years later, I'm not sure what it was.

That's what happened to Nicky and that was the beginning of all of the other bad things that happened in my life.

8

I haven't thought about Nicky in a long time and I'm still afraid to let my mind go there, but this place, this beautiful town on the lake, haunts me whenever I visit.

If I ever do get a cabin in the woods, it probably won't be here. There are too many memories. Too many bad things have happened here. I try to put him out of my mind, but as I get back to my car, start the engine, and drive down the dark road with nothing but headlights in my field of vision, all I see is his face.

When it first happened, I was obsessed with reading his online journal. There was a popular journaling website called *LiveJournal*, where you can make a screen name or use your real name and write about your life.

This was before social media or anything like that. Nicky had an account and one day when we had too much Mountain Dew and sat around giggling and laughing, watching the movie *Scream*, he told me about it.

He just came right out and said that he started a journal and that he didn't want me to read it, but maybe I will someday.

He made me promise that I would never read it, not as long as he was alive and I now wonder whether he had any premonitions that he would not live long.

I wondered a lot about that, but now I think that's just one of those things that teenagers say. You like to think of people around you and what they would do and say about you if you weren't around anymore.

Nicky and I were very macabre in that way. That's why when I went to his funeral, I felt a spirit there, watching, hanging around, seeing who showed up and who didn't. It made me smile. I missed him so much.

Knowing that about him, I felt his presence there.

What did I find on his *LiveJournal*? Not too much.

It had the expected musings about fights with his parents, and how much he missed his dog who ran away and was later found dead after being hit by a car.

I had promised him that I wouldn't read his journal and I managed to keep my promise for a year. After that, I couldn't hold on much longer.

I needed his words to be with me. I needed to feel his presence.

The last entry mentioned me. Well, there were plenty that mentioned me in passing, as his best friend.

Kaitlyn did this and Kaitlyn said that. Kaitlyn is obsessed with Scream, but I don't like it as much. I prefer The Crow. We like to think of ourselves as emo-goth kids without all the black makeup and the black hair comb overs. We listened to metal, we watched 90s horror movies, and we thought that we were deeper than everyone else who wore their highlighter green outfits and sparkles in their hair.

The last journal entry was written the day before his death, the night of, to be more specific.

He mentions me.

He mentions our kiss, describing it in detail.

Sunlight beamed against her tan skin. Her pouty lips opened slightly and I couldn't stay away.

Her big green eyes smiled at me and our fingers intertwined in that way that they never have before. There was a moment right before our lips touched when our childhood seemed to have melted away, just like that.

We were not yet thirteen, but we were no longer children. We had feelings for each other that we couldn't explain, but we could only express when I kissed her.

She tasted of summer, Jolly Ranchers, sunshine, and the big blue lake where we grew up.

Tomorrow I'm going to kiss her again, if she'll let me, and I will ask her to be mine.

I swallow hard, going over the words in my mind. I have read that journal entry thousands of times and the words have imprinted on me.

He wanted to be a writer. He loved writing about his life. He loved putting himself onto paper.

I loved that about him. He would read me excerpts from Wordsworth and Yeats, poems that made my hair stand up on end.

We never talked about it in public, not at school or anything like that. I mean, people knew that he liked to write.

He worked on the newspaper with me and he edited the literary journal, but his interest in poetry was something that he shared only with me.

As I pull up to my mom's house, I wonder what the world missed out on when it lost Nicholas Bender: how much beauty, love, and sorrow.

I also wonder about how much I have lost as the girl who loved him.

I see Luke's rental car in my mom's driveway. I'm both excited and a little bit anxious.

Why is he here?

I park on the street and walk up to the front door, knocking once.

Luke answers the door. He smiles at me and I immediately relax. If they found her body, found something, or even had bad news of any kind, his face would be different.

Luke has big, kind eyes and a casual demeanor that makes him look comfortable in a suit as well as sweatpants. His shoulders are broad and strong.

His hair is getting a little long, but in that attractive, sexy way along with that five o'clock shadow that's really probably three days old. I haven't known him for too long, but I've noticed that he can't really grow a beard.

He gives me a warm hug and I embrace him back.

This is the first time that we have touched since our fight. Mom comes out of the kitchen holding a tray of cookies, freshly baked from the oven.

"Well, this is unusual," I say, giving her a brief hug.

She's a thin-lipped woman who likes to wear her hair pressed tightly to her head.

She's not one to show her emotions around strangers, but recently, around me, she hasn't been able to hold them back much at all. Mom has always been a very put-together kind of woman with strict rules about what should and shouldn't happen.

Curse words were allowed in books as long as they were used appropriately, not gratuitously, and worked with the particular characters, but the number of books which had profanity that she approved of were limited to probably four or five.

She was always partial to fiction written in third person and loved Hawthorne and Faulkner with their elaborate language thick with metaphors.

She did not like the teenage vampire romance trend, but she was happy that it was making kids come into the library and read. At the end, she was a librarian and any reading was better than none as far as she was concerned.

I grab a cookie, take a bite, and am pleasantly surprised. I don't know if it's a result of her love for books and literature in general, but she was never the type to take homemaking very seriously.

She didn't really like to cook or clean, let alone bake.

"Wow, these are delicious," I say, swallowing one and then quickly grabbing another.

"Thank you. Your friend Luke helped me with them."

"You did?" I ask.

He nods.

The jacket from his suit is draped over the wooden chair in the makeshift dining room/office. My mom cleaned up most of her papers and put them in a big pile on one of the bookshelves, but they're not exactly out of the way.

The house is small and every time I come back, it feels smaller than I remember. Ever since Violet had disappeared, something about it has become completely minuscule.

"I had some time," Luke says, "waiting for you to get here and I wanted to ask your mom some questions about Violet anyway, so..."

"So, you figured that you'd come here and bake cookies?" I ask, reaching for my third.

Mom winks at me and says, "Why don't you have a seat? I'll get some tea."

She doesn't offer me dinner and I don't expect it, as it looks like they've already had some.

There's an empty pizza box on the counter that she folds up and stashes next to the recycling bin. Recycling has always been taken very seriously in our household.

My mom carefully sorts all the food and makes sure that the right type of plastic goes into the recycling bin because, as you know, only plastics labeled with a number one and two are easily recyclable, while others, four through seven, are generally not.

The ones listed with a number three, like PVC pipes and children's and pets' toys as well as clamshell containers that are common with takeout food, contain toxins and thus cannot be recycled.

"You know, your friend Luke here is quite an expert on baking cookies," Mom says.

"Yeah, I would say so," I agree. "These oatmeal chocolate chip ones are to die for."

He winks at me while admitting, "My mom is a great baker. She bakes for any reason whatsoever. Christmas, birthdays, Valentine's Day, Presidents' Day."

"Really?"

"Yep. One year when I was in school, I brought in cookies for the whole day for Martin Luther King Day."

"What grade?" I laugh.

He laughs, too, and says, "Fifth. It made me quite popular with the girls if I may say so myself."

I can just imagine, with a lot of cringe, what it would be like for the ten-year-old me to bring in cookies for the whole class. I remember I was embarrassed to even give out Valentine's Day cards, but Luke doesn't seem bothered.

"She actually started up her own bakery," Luke says.

"Where is that?" Mom asks.

"Wichita, Kansas, where I'm from. She was an accountant and she retired, but didn't really like being retired, so she decided to rent this little space on Main Street and started a bakery. It's doing well. They're totally booked up. Birthday parties, wedding cakes, that kind of thing. She has to expand, probably to another location and hire more help, but she just loves doing all the work herself. Kind of a control freak, but in a good way," he jokes.

I give him a smile. This is the first time he's ever talked about his family or anything personal like that and I really appreciate it.

I take another bite of my cookie and revel in the sweet oatmeal goodness. Mom pours us some tea and then says that she's had a long day and is going to go to bed.

"I have the room all set up for you. New sheets, new everything," she says to me. Then she turns to Luke. "It was nice to meet you. Thank you for stopping by, Agent Luke Gavinson."

"No, thank you," he says.

She gives us each a hug and then walks away down the small corridor to the first bedroom on the left.

The floorboards creak in the living room as the house settles all around, but as soon as she steps on the shaggy caramel carpet in the corridor, the house seems to settle and everything's all right again.

Luke and I sit across from each other in the dining room, each holding our cup of tea and occasionally sneaking glances. This is probably the best time to talk about the fight that we had before I left here last time, but neither of us wants to bring it up.

I play with the string of the ginger lemongrass teabag, pulling it in and out of the mug before finally looking up at Luke and asking him about his date.

"That wasn't a real date. I told you that," he says, narrowing his eyes. His voice is quiet but stern. "My cousin set it up. She was there, introducing me to her friend. I promised to go before we met."

"I know. I'm just joking," I say with a casual shrug.

"I don't know why you're getting so upset. It's not like we're dating anyway," he says.

I nod. That part is true.

"I'd like to."

His words catch me by surprise. I look up and he stares deep into my eyes and I can't look away.

"What are you talking about?" I ask, not quite certain if he's joking although everything about his body language says that he's not.

9

I don't really want to talk about this, but I don't have much of a choice. Luke stares at me, waiting for an answer.

"Do you really want to be exclusive?" I ask. "I mean, didn't we just meet not too long ago?"

"Yes, but when you know, you know, right?"

I nod.

"I guess not," he mumbles.

I look up at him, our eyes meet, and I feel like I have done something wrong.

The truth is that I do want to be with him. I do want to call him my boyfriend, but for some reason, I can't. I can't make myself nor do I really want to force it.

"What about your date?" I ask. "It didn't go well?"

"It was a blind date arranged by someone who doesn't really know me."

"She's your cousin, right?"

"Why are you trying to make this something that it's not?" he asks. "You know that it was just a social obligation."

"Why are you coming back here and asking me to be your girlfriend all of a sudden?"

"I thought that we had a good time. I thought that we got along well and I like being with you. Is that a crime?"

"No, of course not." I back down. "I just don't think that I'm ready. I don't think we are ready."

"What do you mean?"

"Well, I ran into my old boyfriend and we had dinner, drinks."

"Dinner or drinks?" he pushes me, narrowing his eyes.

"Drinks, okay?"

"So, what does that mean?"

"Nothing except that I went out with him because I was angry with you and I'm just not sure that's a great foundation for a relationship."

"It's not."

Neither of us say anything for a while, until the silence becomes almost unbearable.

I'm not sure where to go from here and neither is he, but I'm also a little bit annoyed, angry.

We had a fight, but we had a good thing going.

We got along. We had fun and I haven't had fun for a long time.

"Can we just rewind?" I finally ask.

"Rewind to what?"

"Rewind this whole thing. This whole cascade of events. I just want to go back to how things were. Like how we meet up in your motel room, had a good time, and had a few laughs. Why can't we go back to that? Why do we have to put this relationship into a box?"

"We don't," Luke says. "We don't have to do anything."

"So, can we go back?"

"No," he says, shaking his head.

"I don't think I can do that either."

"Why?"

"I don't know. We don't even know each other. I mean, not even as friends, not as anything. So I just can't. I'm just not ready. With everything else that's going on in my personal life, with Violet missing, I just can't take it any further right now."

"Okay, I understand," he says with a nod, but it feels like he doesn't. "Well, it was nice to see you again, Kaitlyn." He pauses for a little bit before saying my first name and I almost feel like he's thinking about whether or not he should call me Detective Carr.

"Don't leave. Don't leave us like this," I plead, but he gets up from behind the table, grabs his coat, and walks out.

I follow him out onto the porch and call out his name again.

"Listen, I'm not taking anything personally," Luke says, turning around right before opening his car door. "Let's just be friends, okay? This is me rewinding things, starting new."

"Okay," I say, holding myself by my shoulders, uncertain as to whether or not I believe him. "Okay, I'll see you tomorrow."

He gets into the car and pulls out. A little bit of snow has fallen since I got here and the driveway's slick.

He's not used to driving in these conditions and he turns against the ice when he should be letting go of the brake and driving with it.

I stay on the porch for a little bit after that, wishing, once again, that this could have gone a little bit differently.

Finally, when the snow starts nipping on my nose a little bit too much, I reach for the door and go inside.

The following morning, I meet up with my mom with a big box of fresh donuts and a jug of coffee.

I'm bringing it over for all of the volunteers who are gathered at the Veterans Hall. There's going to be another press conference at the police station followed by another search around the observatory area.

We drive over to the station, the glaze from the Krispy Kreme covers my fingers and my lips. I'm not much of a donut kind of girl. I love them and pretty much anything sweet, but I try to stay away because they inevitably spike my blood sugar, leaving me tired, hungry, and irritated.

I get to the press conference right on time, just as Captain Talarico takes the podium. Dressed in one of his nicest suits, he looks confident and competent delivering the difficult news.

In addition to finding Violet's clothes packed neatly in a bag, they also find Natalie's clothes packed in the exact same manner, a large plastic bag.

Why?

Why would anyone ask them to strip and then take the time to carefully put everything they were wearing in a bag like that?

I stand near the back of the room and I hear a few deputies gossiping. One of them tells the other about how distraught Natalie's mom was when she heard the news and when she had to identify the clothing as the things that her daughter wore that night.

To say that she was inconsolable would be a grave understatement.

Out by the podium, a little bit against the wall, I see Natalie's brothers, the rest of the triplet set. Steven and Michael stand with their backs against the wall, dressed in similar khaki pants and button-down shirts.

They're here to do some press interviews, no doubt, but they look practically comatose.

I bite my lower lip as I try to decide what to do.

Do I approach them? Do I talk to them now?

Captain Talarico gathers his papers after going over all of the major details in the cases and talking about their possible relationship. I say possible because nothing is certain, but is anyone really not convinced that the two cases aren't related?

They went missing just a few days apart.

They disappeared under very, very similar circumstances.

They were both dropped home in front of their houses, at which point, they went missing.

Nobody has heard from them since and the only evidence that has been collected are the two plastic bags full of everything that they wore.

"Hey, can I talk to you two for a second?" I say, walking up to the boys.

"You're Violet's sister," Michael says, narrowing his eyes immediately.

"Yes, I am, but I'm also a detective and I just want to ask you a few things."

"No," Steven says, shaking his head.

He's a little bit bigger in size than Michael with a doughier face, but kinder eyes.

"Please, I think it would be best if we worked together, if we could compare stories."

"There's nothing to compare. My sister had nothing to do with your sister's disappearance."

This takes me by surprise.

"What are you talking about?" I ask. "Of course the two cases are related. What about the clothes that they found in the park?"

Michael shakes his head and Steven follows along.

"What about the fact that they both went missing in a very similar and suspicious way?"

Michael shakes his head.

"What do you think happened to your sister then?" I ask.

"Nothing. I don't know. I don't know what to think."

"You're certain that her case has nothing to do with Violet's though? Why?"

"Why would they be connected? Why would Natalie run away with Violet?"

"Wait, what?" This really takes me by surprise.

Michael tries to shush him, but Steven is too much on a roll.

"Our sister was one of the most popular girls at school. She and Violet, they just ran in different circles and there's no way they would have run away together."

"Run away together? Why do you think that Natalie *ran away*?" I ask.

"What do you think, there's some sort of serial killer kidnapping teenage girls, making them strip off their clothes, putting them in bags, and leaving them behind?"

That thought has occurred to me, I want to say, but I keep my mouth shut. Steven starts to walk away, but I follow him.

"Can you tell me what you're thinking? What do *you* think happened to Natalie?"

"I don't know what happened, okay, but she told me that she was running away. She even wrote it in an email to me."

"She did?" My mouth nearly drops open.

He pulls out his phone and flashes it to me. I take it carefully, handling it as if it were a bomb, holding my breath as I read it.

I'm not going to be around much longer. Take care of each other and tell Mom not to worry. I'll be fine. I know what I'm doing. I'll be in touch as soon as I get there.

"Get where?" I ask.

He shakes his head.

"You have to tell me."

"I don't know." Steven grabs his phone out of my hand. "This email arrived last night."

My eyes widen. He thinks this is actually an email from Natalie.

"Natalie ran away, okay? She wants to be gone. She had all these problems with my mom and she had all these issues with Neil."

"What about her clothes?" I ask.

"I don't know. Maybe she changed, maybe she knew that we'd all be looking for her. Who knows."

I nod.

Mrs. D'Achille comes over and pulls her sons away from me. I swallow hard as I let the wave of emotion rush through me.

For a moment there, I thought that Steven had actual evidence that she was gone, that maybe she wrote that email before she went missing, but I'm pretty certain that whomever took her wrote that email to throw us off the mark.

He can convince a teenage boy, but not a seasoned professional.

After talking to the boys, I head straight to Captain Talarico and tell him what Steven D'Achille has on his phone.

"The kid thought that he was protecting his sister by covering it up."

As soon as he sees the captain and me approach him, he gets angry.

"I should have never told you a thing!" he yells.

"What are you talking about?"

"This is a message from Natalie."

"Steven, please. We have to go through the proper channels. Our crime tech team has to go through all of your emails and track who sent that email and why."

"No, it's Natalie. I'm certain of it, even the way she signed it and all in her little phrasing. It's her," he insists.

This makes me pause. In fact, it might actually be good news.

"Whether or not it's her, we have to confirm it. It may be her and this may be a clue to finding out where she is."

"What if she doesn't want to be found?"

"That's not really up to her," Captain Talarico says. "She's underage. She can't go missing. Okay?"

"She's going to be so mad at me," Steven mumbles. "I should have never said anything."

When the captain starts to pull him away, I lean over and whisper into his ear.

"I'm glad that you said something. She may be alive and she may need your help. This way we'll find out for sure. If she did run away, well, I'm sure she'll like to know just what kind of caring and loving brother she has watching out for her."

He shakes his head and turns away, reluctantly handing his phone over to one of the deputies holding an evidence bag.

10

R ight after the press conference ends, Mom excuses herself to go to work and I meet up with her later around lunchtime.

Work is her sanctuary. It's her happy place, just like it is for me.

She likes being around books. She likes organizing them, handling them, getting new ones in, and cataloging them.

I park out front of the public library, where I have spent many happy hours of my life. The building is rather bureaucratic in its formality, no columns or fancy things like they have in some big city libraries, but more like an office building with a no-nonsense exterior and even less no-nonsense interior.

I find Mom in the back, walking around with a trolley, sorting. She only works here part time now, just because more hours are not available, but I have a sneaky suspicion that she would work here for free if she could.

I tell her about what happened with Natalie's brothers and she sighs loudly at the end.

"That's not her writing that email," she says quietly.

"No, I don't think so either, but we're going to confirm. Maybe it was her typing it out and she's somewhere and they left some sort of online ID."

"So, you'll be able to track the location of whomever wrote that?"

"Yeah, unless they took steps to cover up their cyber trail, which is not unheard of, of course."

"So, you're certain that the two of them are together?" Mom asks.

"I'm not certain of anything. This is probably the strangest case that I've ever worked." I shake my head and whisper, "I don't know what the connection is between them. I mean, they're friends. They go to the same school, but why take both of them? The thing that makes it particularly difficult is that it's a stranger or someone who is almost a stranger, which makes it very hard for investigators to track."

"What do you mean?" Mom sticks her hands into her pockets.

"Well, you know, if it's someone that Violet knows directly, that's one thing, though I'm not sure that either of them know this person. In most criminal cases, it's a close family member or friend, usually a male. It's in their circle of friends, so to speak, so it's easy to connect the dots or easier. DNA and all the other forensic evidence helps that along, but in this case, we don't have any forensic evidence. We don't have a body. We don't even have a circle of friends that this could be tied to or he could be tied to and that's what makes it quite difficult."

"It's still going to be solved, right?"

I nod and promise that it will, but she and I both know that I can't make that kind of promise.

In my line of work, I tend to make promises that I really shouldn't. But how do I say no though?

I always promise that I will find out the truth, but what I'm really promising is that I'll do my best and this case is no different.

I will do my best to find out what happened to Natalie and to my sister. I will do my best to try to find out the truth and I'll keep working this case for as long as possible, long after everyone else gives up.

A coworker walks by, looking back occasionally with a lot of nervousness in her body. Mom says hello to her, but their interaction is terse and quick.

"What was that?" I ask my mom.

She just shrugs and looks past her coworker. The tone of the afternoon seems to shift. She doesn't have to tell me because I already know.

When you're family to someone who's gone missing or a murder victim, people don't know what to say to you. People don't know how to act around you. After the initial condolences and asking for details about what's going on, a wall takes over.

To change the topic, Mom invites me out to lunch and we can't get there fast enough. We drive to one of our favorite restaurants in town. It's relatively modern and it has a serious LA vibe, lots of specialty cocktails as well as ahi tuna for appetizers. Mom insists that it's going to be her treat. As soon as we order a round of cocktails, I find out why.

"I hate to ask you, but I need to borrow some money," she says directly, without beating around the bush.

I'm actually a little bit surprised. She has always been very responsible and good with finances.

"I'm behind on the mortgage. I've had some unexpected expenses creep up. Violet's braces, things like that and I just don't get paid that much."

"Yes, I understand. Anything you need. How much?" I ask after a pause.

My grapefruit vodka cocktail arrives and I take a few big gulps to try to ease some of the anxiety of being here and having this conversation. I don't know if you know what it's like to have your parent ask you for money, but it doesn't feel good.

Despite my dad's illegal activities and all of their problems when I was growing up, Mom always made sure that the mortgage was paid and everything was taken care of.

I didn't live a lavish life, but I was also never worried about being evicted or thrown out onto the street. I actually had no idea that was what really happened until after I graduated.

"Is everything okay, Mom?" I ask, after she finishes one cocktail and orders another.

"I like that guy, Luke, the FBI agent, your friend."

"Yes, of course." I nod, taking a bite of the pita chip.

"He seemed like he'd be good for you."

"Yeah, I guess."

"What do you think?" she asks.

"I don't know. I mean, I enjoy spending time with him, but it's complicated."

"Doesn't sound like it's very complicated. I heard him say that he wants to be with you."

"Were you spying on us?"

"No, of course not, but the walls in the house are thin, as you know."

I nod thinking back to all the fights that I overheard her have with Dad and how loud Violet was when she cried as a baby.

"Why did you say no?" Mom asks. "He seems to be like the type of guy who would be appreciative of your line of work and wouldn't be scared by all the hours you put in."

"Yeah, I guess," I mumble, taking another bite.

"Tell me what you're thinking, Kaitlyn."

I swallow hard. It's hard for me to explain.

"I don't know. I wasn't really thinking anything. I'm not ready," I finally say.

"Are you not ready or are you scared? Those two things are not the same."

"Why are we talking about this? Why don't we talk about Violet?"

"There's nothing to say about Violet," Mom says. "Besides I need to talk about something else. I need to think about something else. Otherwise, I might lose my mind."

I reach over and grab the glass of water, bring it to my lips, and feel the chill of the ice cubes on my tongue.

"I just don't know if I can date like that. I mean, he wanted me to be his girlfriend. He wanted us to be exclusive, but I don't know what that means."

"That means you don't date anyone else. You see each other. You spend time with one another. You see if you can put up with one another long enough to spend a few years together. If that goes well, you get married," Mom says, tossing her hair from one side to another.

"That's so romantic." I laugh.

"Listen, I believe in love, you know? Real deep, all consuming love, but I also believe that this is what it requires. It requires you to take a chance to jump."

"I don't have a parachute," I say.

"You don't need one."

"You always need a parachute if you jump from a high place."

Our eyes meet and she shakes her head.

"Why do you think I was together with your father all of those years long after I knew that he was selling drugs and he was running one of the biggest operations in this part of California?"

It's the first time she's ever spoken to me about him like that.

"Why?" I ask.

"Despite all of it, despite that secret life, despite all the danger that he put himself in and he put our family in, I loved him and I wanted to be with him. I didn't need a parachute because I knew that it would be okay."

I bite the inside of my cheek.

"It wasn't okay, Mom," I say. "You needed a parachute because he was killed. You found him dead in your room with two gunshot wounds in the stomach. You needed a parachute to protect you from all of that pain and to protect us from all of that sadness."

"No, I didn't need one," Mom says. "Just because something bad happened at the end, doesn't mean that we didn't have a million beautiful, amazing moments together."

"Yes, it would mean that," I say after a long pause. "I mean, I love Dad, of course, but you were the one who was married to him."

"The thing about it, Kaitlyn, is that you don't not read a book just because it's going to end badly. You read it anyway. You read it despite that. If you think about it, everything in life ends badly, right? We all die. We all have to say goodbye."

"No," I say quickly. "I don't believe that. I mean, yes, we all die, but we don't all have to die like that. We don't have to be murdered."

"Don't say that," she hisses, putting her finger in my face. "He was not murdered. He killed himself."

"You don't know that."

She looks away from me, pursing her lips. She tries to hold back tears.

"I don't want to fight about this, Mom. Let's just agree to disagree, but no, not all deaths are a sign that everything ends badly. The majority of them are a sign of a life well lived. Besides, I tend to believe in another pearl of wisdom as they say that I think it's an Indian saying that goes something like everything is okay in the end and if it's not okay, it's not the end."

Our food arrives and we sit together silently after the waitress leaves, not looking at each other, but not diving right in as well. It's a moment of contemplation of thought.

Somewhere in the distance, a bird chirps and dances on a twig. One car pulls out and another pulls in.

A group of girls walk by giggling and a young father carries his toddler on his shoulders licking an ice cream cone.

We spend the rest of lunch talking about things that don't really matter. She doesn't bring up Luke and I don't bring up my father.

Neither of us mention Violet. Sometimes you have to consciously avoid certain topics in order to just get through it.

Just as the check arrives, Mom insists, "I'm paying for it."

I'm quickly reminded of the fact that she just asked me to borrow money for the mortgage.

How many months behind is she? How much does she need?

What happens if I can't help her out in a few months?

As she signs and gives a generous tip, I notice how very put together she looks now in comparison to how she did before. It throws me off a little bit.

My mom is kind of like a chameleon who takes on personas. She becomes different people or maybe she's just trying like the rest of us.

Maybe she just has her good days and her bad and that's okay.

11

I've been dreading this moment for a while, but it's something that has to be done. I meet Luke outside of Natalie's family house. I park right behind his rented Toyota, knock on the windshield, and get in to go over what we want to ask him.

I'm not officially on the case and the fact that I'm here at all is a courtesy. I have updated him about what happened with Michael and Steven. He's unhappy with the fact that I talked to them on my own.

He is, however, eager to get back the results of the email and the IP address that it could lead to. It takes a special kind of knowledge to make your communications over email and the internet in general secret, really secret from professionals.

"Listen, I want to apologize about what happened yesterday."

"No, please don't," Luke says, going over his notes in his journal.

"What do you mean?" I ask.

"Please do not. Let's not talk about that. I really need to focus and we have to get this interview right."

I nod.

"You shouldn't even be here, but I think that you might be able to elicit something from her brothers," he says.

It's pretty clear to me that he is avoiding meeting my eyes. His journal opens down the middle and fits in the palm of his hand. The pages are blank, unlined, but filled up with his unorganized scrawl.

The lettering is small and it's difficult to read, but occasionally there are spots where he kept the pen on too long, probably thinking about something and it bled through to the other side.

The energy inside Natalie's house feels different from before. Detectives and people in law enforcement in general like to pretend or like to say that their work is very objective.

The part where you talk to the victim's parents and you interview people in their life is anything but that. This involves assessing people's credibility, figuring out why they're saying what they're saying.

Are they telling the truth?

That begins with that gut feeling you get walking into a place where you've been before and feeling that somehow everything is different.

Tension seems to hang in the air, filling up the house all the way to the top of the cathedral ceilings. Natalie's mom isn't particularly too pleased to see me, but she doesn't say anything to that effect.

I let Luke do all the talking. I let him take the lead because this isn't my case at all. He takes a seat across from her at the dining room table with a big decal above the wall that reads 'Believe'.

There are a few crosses in the living room, as well as a few other paintings, pictures, and decals that read 'Faith' and 'Home'.

It's not the religious symbols that make me feel uncomfortable. It's something else. Mrs. D'Achille looks at me in that suspicious way that you do when you don't approve of something or somebody.

Usually relatives try to find people who can relate to their situation and given the fact that my sister has also gone missing, I find her reaction to be unusual and surprising.

We've already exchanged words and things were different then. There was an openness to her that is now gone. It's almost as if she blames me or perhaps Violet for what has happened to her daughter.

I give Luke and her some space when I ask if I can get a cup of water in the kitchen. She points me in the direction and that's where I see Michael again.

"I'm sorry about earlier," he says.

"No problem at all." I nod. "I just want to speak to you about anything that you want to speak about. I know that Steven believes that she ran away, but that email came yesterday."

"Yes. Steven thinks that she left on her own because that's what he wants to think and that's what I'm going to let him think," Michael says, looking down at his knuckles; he makes a fist and then looks up at me glaring. "You don't think that at all?"

"What do you know?"

He doesn't respond.

I ask him again, "What is it that you're trying to tell me?"

"Nothing."

"Michael, if you know anything, you have to tell me. Any little bit of information, you never know where it's going to lead. You never know what kind of things it will uncover. Natalie was very private. She wouldn't want anything out and we're going to maintain whatever you unveil in secret, but the authorities have to know. I have to know in order to help you find your sister, do you understand?"

He shifts his weight from one side to another, still hesitating.

He doesn't trust me. I don't blame him. I'm not officially on the case and my sister is missing as well.

I lean a little bit closer and open my mouth to say something else, but I can feel his body shutting down.

The next words out of my mouth need to be significant, otherwise I might lose him forever.

"I promise you that I'm going to keep everything you tell me at utmost secrecy. I will only reveal it to the police if I feel like it's relevant."

I have no right to say any of this. This is against protocol. I have no idea whether or not anything's relevant until you put all the pieces of the puzzle together.

I need him to tell me what he's keeping secret.

He hesitates again.

Finally, he says, "I found a video. It's a secret YouTube video. She made it private. Then it required a password to open, but she only uses like two or three passwords total. So, I saw it on her account."

"What kind of video?" I ask.

"Just videos of her talking about her life, saying how much she wants to cut off her hair and color it purple."

"Oh, okay. That's not unusual, right? That doesn't seem outrageous?" I say.

"It is according to my mother, our mother. She's not exactly the most understanding person. She was obsessed with Natalie being perfect. When her hair started to turn darker like ours, she insisted that she color it and go get highlights. She makes her go every six weeks, even though Natalie couldn't care less. For a while, she wouldn't let her wear makeup. Then she relented and insisted that she only wear the most perfect kind. She wanted her to get her face contoured."

"Contoured?" I ask.

"I don't know, like you spray on foundation and powder in a particular way. I think it gives you higher cheekbones and a smaller nose. I don't know; there's all this stuff on YouTube about it."

"Natalie didn't want that?"

"No. She wanted to shave the back of her head. She wanted to color her hair purple. She wanted to paint her nails black. She just wanted to be *different*. She didn't want to be Mom approved."

"So, is that what she talked about in these videos?"

"Yeah."

"Okay. Would you mind giving me access to them?"

"Sure."

"Does your brother know about them?"

"Yes, he does. We knew everything that she was going through. Mom wanted her to be the most popular girl at school because that's what she missed out on when she was a kid. Now Natalie didn't want anything to do with that. She didn't want to be a cheerleader. She didn't want everyone to know who she was. She was just very good at playing that role."

He pulls up the videos and shows them to me after putting in the password.

"Can you send them to me?" I ask. "I need to be able to watch all of them more than once."

"Yeah, that's fine," he says. "Please don't tell our mom, our dad, or anyone that you don't really have to."

He hands me the phone and I start looking through the videos. He hesitates a little bit.

"What's wrong?" I ask.

"Nothing. I'm just waiting for you to find that."

"Find what?" I realize that it's going to be very difficult for me to watch these videos while he's here.

"Click on the fourth video and go to the timestamp five minutes twenty-five seconds."

I do as he says and that's when I see it.

My mouth drops open.

12

I lean over Michael's shoulder to get a good look of his screen. He holds the phone slightly toward him away from me, almost as if he wants to both share what's on it and to shield me from what I'm about to see.

When he fast forwards to the right spot, I see Natalie sitting across from Violet.

In Violet's room the camera is set up so that it's at eye level. They're sitting on the floor with the pink bedspread behind them as a backdrop.

Natalie laughs.

The sound of her laughter reverberates around the walls, wood paneled and then painted over in a matte, but white, and covered up with cut-outs from magazines.

There is a vision board hanging somewhere in the distance between them. Pristine white beaches with tall palm trees swaying in the wind with a laptop with YouTube on the front.

I'm assuming that one of her goals is to start a YouTube channel, something she has talked about for a long time.

Out in the corner are tall pines and a lake, a familiar view of Big Bear.

Underneath, the word 'home' hangs in the air, written in a farmhouse style.

Violet looks small in comparison to Natalie, meek. Her hair isn't as shiny or lustrous, but rather flat.

It looks like it hasn't been brushed or washed for a day or two. Natalie looks, well, beautiful, but elusive. Her hair is that elusive ash blonde, cool and flattering. Her skin is sun-kissed and just a little bit golden brown.

These two girls look like they would have nothing in common and not spend any time with each other at school, yet watching them silently gaze into each other's eyes and talk about nothing in particular, I can tell that they have feelings for one another.

"I think I'm going to love you forever," Violet says.

The sentence comes out of nowhere, but it doesn't seem to take Natalie by surprise.

Instead, she just reaches over and kisses her. It's a small peck, delicate.

The kind that tells you that this isn't the first time they have touched one another. Then Natalie reaches over and tucks a hair behind Violet's ear. Violet leans over to kiss her again.

I realize that this video may only be made for private viewing, but I continue watching because I have to know what happens. Maybe there is a clue to their disappearance.

They start to laugh again. Natalie points to her nails and Violet gets out a sparkly pink nail polish that Natalie shakes her head at.

"No, absolutely not." She laughs, reaching over and grabbing the black one. "This one."

"So, what did you want to show me exactly?" I ask Michael. "The kiss?"

He looks at me dumbfounded and explains, "Of course!"

"Of course, what?" I ask.

"Of course the kiss. I mean, they're like together."

It suddenly occurs to me that he knows nothing about those other videos with Neil, the ones that Violet had on her computer.

"So, do you think that Violet and Natalie were together, *romantically?*"

"I always thought that Neil was her boyfriend. They dated on and off, but then I found these videos and now I have no idea. I didn't even know that she and Violet were friends."

I nod.

"I know that you're from LA and probably seeing two girls kissing is not a big deal to you and I'm very aware of the fact that it's probably not a big deal in general, but in our family things are different. There are certain expectations."

"Tell me about them," I say.

"My parents, they're just really tough on her. They expect her to be this perfect daughter and she's not really like that. She doesn't like to dress up in pretty dresses. She doesn't like to have her hair that color, but Mom is insistent. Mom wants her to be the teenager that she never got to be."

"What do you mean?" I ask.

"Well, Mom got pregnant senior year. She wasn't ever really that popular and she just wants to relive everything through us. She wants us to do high school right."

"You're not even in high school," I say.

"I know, but she's getting us ready for that. She's preparing us for all of these things that are going to happen, all of these ways that we have to act that I'm not really sure what Natalie will be able to."

I want to ask him why he gets so mad at Steven for basically telling me the exact same thing earlier, but we're interrupted by the sound of footsteps somewhere on the other side of the wall.

"I just wanted to show you this so that you'd know. I don't know if it has anything to do with anything, but please don't share this with my parents unless absolutely necessary."

"I promise that I won't."

"This would just break their hearts and I don't want them to stop looking for Natalie. I don't want them to reject her or think that whatever happened to her, she deserves it."

"They would do that?" I ask.

"They're very firm about their beliefs."

I hear another clickety-clack of footsteps getting closer to us. I quickly ask him for the login information and if he can send me the videos to my Dropbox.

I can see him hesitating, but he agrees.

"You really have to be careful with this," he says. "I can tell that you don't think it's a big deal, but it is. My parents are very traditional and religious to like the ninth degree. They wouldn't even let Natalie cut her hair short. So, you can imagine what they would say if they saw her kissing a girl."

I nod and promise to keep this safe and exclusively on a need-to-know basis.

LATER THAT AFTERNOON, Luke and his team bring Neil and his father in for questioning. This has been the interview that they have been preparing for.

"Given the fact that Neil's father is a prosecutor and knows the complete ins and out of the system, it's important to treat him with a delicate touch," Luke says while we grab some coffee at the vending machine. I had offered to run out and get some at a real coffee shop, but he declined.

"I'm used to drinking this cold, crappy brew." Then he kind of puts me at ease. "If you know what I mean?"

I nod. I know exactly what he means.

I have discovered that there is certain things that I always do in repetition in order to prepare for an interrogation.

It's not so much for superstitious purposes, it's more to put me at ease in asking uncomfortable questions.

The thing about being an interviewer is that it's not as simple as appearing to be good cop and bad cop. That's part of it, but there are so many shades of blue in between.

Different suspects require different approaches. Some do better when you're approachable and relatable and polite. Others do better with direct pressure and a good dose of fear mongering.

Neil is a difficult case.

Not only is he a child, which means that he needs to have his parent present, but his father is a district attorney.

That means that he knows exactly what kind of questions and answers would put his son in danger.

I'm not saying that he would cover up a murder, but parents do a lot of stuff for their children and stopping an interrogation would be the least of that.

13

Since I'm not officially on the case, I sit with Captain Talarico and a few other deputies in another room watching everything that's happening on video.

There are a few camera angles set up, one that focuses on Luke and others that are focused on Neil and his father. Mr. Goss is a tall, confident man with broad shoulders and an incredulous smirk on his face that's perfect for Court TV.

His son looks terrified. He sits deep into his chair hanging his head when Luke fumbles with his folders of paperwork, probably on purpose to appear a little bit disorganized and to give them a false sense of security.

Mr. Goss nudges Neil in the ribs to get him to sit up straight and not look so guilty.

"Tell me about your relationship with Natalie," Luke begins.

Neil goes over pretty much the same thing that he has told me and probably all the other investigators on the case.

Luke carefully goes from one question to the next. The interview proceeds slowly, but deliberately.

He goes through all of the questions that he showed me and then some trying to get definitive answers on videotape for the future. There are a few that Mr. Goss opposes to and Neil does not answer.

The majority of them are centered on Neil coming to me in private and telling me that he was out with Violet before, after she got dropped off.

It's clear to me why Mr. Goss doesn't want to talk about this or have any of this on tape. He suspects that his son may be somehow involved.

I'm not saying that he's responsible for her death. I'm not saying that I think that Neil is responsible for Violet's disappearance.

However, the last thing that his father, the prosecutor, wants to do is place him as the last person to officially see Violet.

Luke doesn't let up.

He points out the fact that we found Violet and then later Natalie's clothing in a plastic bag at the exact location where Neil said that he was with Violet the night of her disappearance. Again, his father refuses to let him answer.

"You realize that it was your statement to one of my colleagues about being with Violet at the observatory that led to us finding her clothes?"

"You will not answer that question, Neil," his father barks and then glares at Luke.

"Why is that? You know more than you're saying?" Luke finally presses. He has been dancing around this question for a while, but since the answer is a no, why not press harder?

"I'm going to cut this interview short, Agent Gavinson, if you don't stop accusing my son of having something to do with his friend's disappearance. We're all very sorry about what happened to her, but it's not his fault. You know that. I know that."

"No, I don't know that," Luke says, sitting back in his chair. "All I know is that Violet Carr is missing and your son was the last person to see her alive."

"Please, come on, don't be so dramatic," Mr. Goss pipes in. "I'm not confirming anything that Neil said and I'm not allowing for you to ask him anymore questions. I was here out of courtesy, but that courtesy is now being revoked. I can see that our efforts in helping you with this case are going unappreciated."

"No, we very much appreciate Neil's cooperation," Luke says. "What I don't appreciate, however, are the lies. Your son knows a lot more than he's saying. What I want him to know is that if he cares about his friend Violet at all and if he wants to help us find her, then he would tell us everything that he knows about that night."

"I already told you everything," Neil says. "And Detective Carr. I told her that I picked her up."

"Neil, shut up," Mr. Goss interrupts him, but Neil's eyes are huge like saucers and his cheeks are bright red.

Anger is boiling up within him and he stands up.

He pops up to his feet and puts his face in Luke's face.

"I told Detective Carr everything. I picked her up when she got dropped off by Kaylee and her mom. She waited for me in the driveway. She got on my moped. We drove around. We went all the way to the observatory. We had some food. We made out. That's it, nothing happened."

"Then you dropped her off at home?"

"We're leaving. Let's go," Mr. Goss says, grabbing his son by his shirt and pushing him toward the door.

"I dropped her back off. I have no idea why her clothes were found there."

"Were these the clothes that she was wearing the last time you saw her?" Luke asks, wasting no time.

Mr. Goss keeps trying to usher Neil toward the door, tugging on his arm and physically moving him, but Neil doesn't budge.

"Yes, that's what she was wearing."

"Shut up." He hits the back of his head and Neil winces in pain.

"You did not just do that, did you?" Luke asks, walking up to Mr. Goss and physically getting in between him and Neil. "I will not stand for any physical abuse of children, let alone one that happens right in front of me."

"I wasn't physically abusing my son, you moron," Mr. Goss barks.

"You just hit him in the back of his head right in front of me. You realize that you're not allowed to do that and I'm a mandatory reporter."

"What are you going to do? Call *Child Protective Services* on me?"

"Yes, that would be appropriate," Luke says, crossing his arms. "If you do that in front of an FBI agent in an interview room where you know we are recording every single thing that is being said, who knows what kind of sick and twisted things you're capable of doing in the privacy of your own home. But, that's not for me to find out."

I lean over and take a closer look at Neil who has a small smile on his face.

I have a feeling that very few people have ever stood up to Mr. Goss and it's nice for Neil to see that someone is actually capable of bullying the bully.

"If you think that you can talk to my son while you call CPS to investigate me, you are sorely mistaken. You cannot do that," Mr. Goss says.

"Yes, I know, but that's not why I'm doing it."

He turns to Neil and asks him, "Is there anything else that you can tell me about that night? You dropped her off. Did you really drop her off?"

I bite my lower lip.

I know that he's asking this in front of his father because were Neil to admit something outside of a parent's presence, there is no way that it could be used in court as evidence against him and it would put the whole chain of evidence in jeopardy.

"I just dropped her off," Neil says. "Now I wish I hadn't, but I have no idea how her clothes got back to the observatory, why, or what happened to her. I wish that I could help you. That's why I told her mom and her sister what happened because it doesn't matter if I'm the last person who's seen her alive. I just want her found."

"What do you mean, the last person seen her *alive*?" Luke asks.

"That's it, we're leaving." Mr. Goss pushes his son out the door.

"I just meant that, you know, because she might be dead," Neil relents.

I watch the expression on his face fade and become more distant. It's almost as if he has said too much.

He realizes that he made a mistake and now he needs his father there after all, no matter how much he likes seeing someone put him in his place.

14

I go in to talk to Luke after the Gosses leave. He continues to sit in the interview room, a little dumbfounded with a vacant expression on his face.

"What do you think?" I ask.

He just shakes his head and responds, "I don't know. I thought that he had nothing to do with this for a while. I mean, against all odds, kind of. He seemed to really care and then that last statement at the end just throws me for a loop."

"I know what you mean," I say.

We've all seen it a million times before. A person you interview says all the right things and you start to believe him and you think maybe they didn't do it. At the end, they say something that they couldn't possibly know. They use a past tense. They refer to someone as if they're not there. They refer to someone as dead when they couldn't know for sure. It's a small detail, but it points you in the right direction. In reality, everyone always refers to everyone in present tense until they know for sure that they are no longer with us. Neil Goss didn't do exactly that, but he came close. He referred to Violet as possibly dead, not just missing.

"What are you thinking?" I ask. "Do you think he had something to do with it?"

"He was the last person to see her. He admitted to being there. As far as forensic evidence, I don't know. They're still collecting and you know how it is. It takes a while to get anything back. This isn't television."

"If Neil is guilty, then that means... What does that mean exactly? Would he have killed her or is he still keeping her alive somewhere?" I ask this out loud, letting my mind wander.

"You shouldn't let yourself think like that," Luke says. "I know you're a professional, but she's your sister and it's different when it's family. You know that."

"I know, but what can I do? It's almost like I've been preparing my whole career to deal with this case and I'm not prepared at all."

"You can't be. No one can," Luke says, shaking his head. "It always takes you by surprise. No matter how much we see it happening to other people, we just can't imagine it happening to us."

"It just doesn't seem real," I say and tears start to gather in the back of my eyes. My jaw clenches and that familiar feeling of way too much saliva floods my mouth. I'm so tired, exhausted, and emotionally spent that I can't keep my tears at bay, not even a little bit.

When Luke throws his arms around me, pulls me close, and holds me there, despite me trying to break away, I let myself sob and I really lose myself in the emotion. He holds me as my whole body shakes and I gasp for breath. I wipe the wetness on his jacket, but my face just gets more and more drenched. Somehow when I let my tears start going, I can't make them stop. It was almost easier to keep everything bottled up like it was before. It's safer. Now that they're out, I can't make them stop. I have no more control. I have no control over my body. I have no control over anything.

A few minutes later, when I start to calm down, I try to break awayagain. Again, he stops me and he just holds me. It's like he knows what I need more than I do. I like that. I like the comfort and the security that it makes me feel.

"Are you okay?" he asks, wiping the tears from my cheeks and lifting my head up to his.

I lick my lips since they are inexplicably dry and so is my mouth. It's as if all water within me seemed to have vanished or evaporated.

"I'm sorry about that," I say. "I don't know what came over me."

"It's fine. I understand. This case is so personal. I just wish that you weren't here."

"No, I'm glad that I was," I say. "You didn't bring up the fact that Natalie and Violet were making out."

"Yeah, I didn't. His dad was there and I wasn't sure I was going to get the truth about that. I also didn't want that coming back to Natalie's parents."

"That was the right approach, the right thing to do."

"Of course, but I still wonder what his reaction would be."

When I walk back out into the precinct, everyone is polite enough to not ask me how I'm feeling and I appreciate their concern. There are a few looks of sympathy and support, but that's it. You can always depend on cops to not talk too much about their feelings. In this case, I appreciate that very much. They know what it's like when you lose control of your emotions, especially in the workplace and they know that you need some time to get back to normal. Talking about it is something you do with a therapist, but not with everyone else, at least not unless you are close friends.

Captain Talarico asks to see us in his office and when we arrive, there are a few more agents and deputies there as well. We end up moving to the conference room next door and talk about what happened with the Neil Goss interview. These kinds of meetings allow us to review the footage and talk about why someone is lying, along with where and how. It allows the newer deputies to learn how to identify certain signs, certain emotions, and what decisions have to be made with the investigation as a whole.

"I may be in the minority here," Captain Talarico says. "After we have reviewed all the footage, including the last bit when Mr. Goss was trying to get Neil out of the room as fast as possible, I get the sense that he's telling the truth."

Luke snaps his attention to him with a complete look of surprise on his face.

"Listen, I heard what he said at the end. Don't get me wrong, but I don't know. It just feels like he's telling the truth."

Cops like to talk about their gut a lot. Somehow their gut has become a metaphor for this general intuition or this feeling that you can't describe and you don't have much evidence for, but you still feel. As a professional, we like to pretend that everything is very objective and all decisions are made in this objective way. The truth is that when we talk about our gut, we're talking about our feelings and there is nothing objective about that. This isn't an accusation at all. This job wouldn't be possible without feelings.

In fact, I wish that we would talk about them more in the open with the people we interview, the questions that we ask, and the people we suspect. They require evidence, but it's really the feelings that get us there first. Something doesn't add up, something feels off, something feels like it doesn't quite fit. These hunches, this intuition, these gut reactions, are the source of all that we do. In this case, the captain is arguing exactly what I am feeling.

"Why would he come and talk to Mrs. Carr," Captain Talarico asks, "and put him at the center of this investigation? This is just a question, playing a devil's advocate or whatever, but tell me your thoughts."

This is a brainstorming session. Not all precincts do this, but I like that Captain Talarico does. It brings in input from people that would otherwise not provide any and it allows everyone to learn how to be better investigators.

"You can't deny the fact that he said what he said," Luke says, changing the topic.

"No, of course not, but he knows that she's missing. He knows that this is an investigation. He didn't come out and say that she was dead. He did say possibly dead though."

"Yeah, but still, there is something off about that."

"There is. I'm not going to argue. Let's think about everything else he said in this two hour conversation. It seemed to me that he wanted to be helpful."

"Murderers are often hanging around police stations trying to be helpful. You know that." Luke laughs and so does the captain.

15

We discuss the case in more detail. He argues for the possibility of the girls running away. There isn't much evidence of that, but then again, there isn't much evidence of much else.

It's hard for me to tell if he's playing devil's advocate or just trying to mess with me. The other possibility is that he actually believes that they ran away together.

"What about the clothes?" I ask.

The clothes are a never ending question to just about any possible theory. Why would the clothes be found in two Ziploc bags, folded over, and tucked in pretty neatly?

Why would they do that if they were going to run away?

Why would anyone do that if they took them? Leaving the clothes is leaving evidence.

Currently they're getting checked for fibers, saliva, and every other bodily fluid, but it's going to be a while before we have any of the results even though we put in rush orders.

If someone had taken them, why not just take both of them and disappear completely?

If they ran away, why not just run away wearing the clothes on their back?

It's a mystery that I need to solve, but by the expression on Captain Talarico's face, I can tell that it's something that he's worried we might never get answers to.

"What about money?" I ask. "If they did run away, where did they get money from? They don't have bank accounts. They had debit cards, but there's been no activity on them. How could they pay for anything?"

"I don't know. That's why it's just a possibility," Captain Talarico says.

Luke and I exchange a significant glance. Their theory doesn't make any more sense than mine and, unfortunately, we won't know the truth until we find out more.

Luke and I walk out of Captain Talarico's office and he asks if we can have dinner again.

"I'd like to, but I have to get back," I say. "I have this murder case that I'm working and I'm already really behind."

"What happens if they assign it to someone else?"

"This is my job, Luke. This is what I do for a living. I wouldn't ask you to not take some job somewhere else for me."

"You wouldn't?" he asks.

We're standing in the hallway where people are coming and going. We're keeping our voices hushed, but that only makes us seem more suspicious.

This isn't the right place to have the conversation. He walks me out to my car in the parking lot where we can have a little bit more privacy.

"If you want to be in a relationship with me, don't ask me to put my career on the back burner," I say, crossing my arms. "That's not going to get you anywhere."

"Yeah, I can see that." He nods. "It's not really about your career, is it?"

"I was here for the interviews. I'll be here for another press conference. I have to go back and do my job. Plus, there's only so few things I can do here. You know that."

"What about interviewing all of her school friends, talking to people who work in gas stations, and anyone who's around the comings and goings of this town? You know who works here. You know who lives here. You know who her friends are."

"Please don't try to make me feel guilty. I'm here. I'm here as much as I can be, but one day or two days in LA is not going to change anything. I need to work on that case. If I'm not there, it's going to get assigned to someone else and then who knows what case I'll get next."

We stand looking into each other's eyes for a second.

He doesn't look disappointed, just acknowledging what I'm saying. I can actually see him hearing me, which I appreciate.

A lot of the guys that I've dated before seem to gloss over my needs and wants when I tell them what I have to do and what I can't do.

I know that he still wants me to get serious with him. He still wants me to be his girlfriend, but luckily, he doesn't bring that up.

Luckily, he lets it go and I don't talk about it either. I like this place where we are now.

This friendly ground where he sees me and I see him while there's a possibility of what may happen in the future.

"Kaitlyn!" Mom yells my name from across the parking lot. She waves at me and walks over briskly.

"What's wrong? What are you doing here?" I ask.

"I wanted to catch you since you told me that you were leaving."

"Yeah, but I'll be back. I just have to get back to LA for a bit."

"I need to talk to you," she says quietly.

"Yeah, sure." I give a nod to Luke and he leaves.

Mom is dressed in her favorite plum trench coat and thick boots. She gets cold easily. I guess that's where I get it from since my body starts to shiver even when everyone else is just wearing long sleeves.

Mom has had a thyroid problem for a while and even takes medication for it, but when I got mine checked out, everything turned out to be fine. The cold is just due to my unusually low body temperature.

"Thanks for coming by," I say and wave her over to sit down in my car.

"Yeah, sure. Why do we have to go in here?" she asks and I pull off some of the wrappers from the front seat. "You know, you could clean this car once in a while. It wouldn't kill you."

I roll my eyes or rather resist to fully roll my eyes.

She takes her finger, runs it over the dashboard, and points out, "Look at this, look at how dirty this is."

"Mom, can we not talk about this right now?"

"You know, they have these people called detailers and they'll come over, vacuum your car, and all that stuff."

"It also costs $150 bucks and I would have to stay home, so that's impossible."

"What about running it through the car wash once in a while? That's, what, fifteen dollars?"

"Mom, I just don't have the mental space to deal with washing cars right now. Can we just talk about what you came here to talk about?"

"Sure," she says, disappointed.

She pulls on her coat and sets it on top of her lap, almost not wanting it to touch her seat.

There's trash packed into each of the compartments on both sides and I wish that I took the time to throw it all out before she came here.

"If you were visiting my apartment, I would have invested a little bit in a housekeeper to come out once and get it all ready, but this is a surprise visit. What did you want to talk to me about?" I ask.

"Just if you found out anything else about Violet. Any news on the case? Anything that the cops aren't necessarily sharing with everyone?"

I bite my lower lip.

"Yes, there is something, huh?" She reads me immediately.

It was probably because I already wanted to ask her about it and just didn't know how. Normally, I'm much better at withholding the truth.

I don't know exactly how to ask her this question.

I feel nervous and uneasy. I don't want to tell Mom anything that Violet doesn't want her to know, but at the same time, I need to know what she knows.

"Have you known Violet to ever show any interest in *girls*?" I ask.

"What do you mean by that? What do you mean by *interest*?"

"You know what I mean. Like romantically?"

Mom turns in her seat, stares at me, and asks, "Do you think that Violet was dating a girl?"

"I'm not saying that exactly and at her age I don't know what that even means. Do you think that maybe she had feelings for a girl? Did you ever talk to her about it?"

"No, of course not, but I also never talked to her about dating guys. I had no idea that she was at that stage in her life," Mom says, carefully choosing her words.

I think that my own teenage years traumatized her. I was a bit of a wild child.

I went out a lot. I did what I wanted.

I hooked up with guys that I wanted. I figured that if guys got to do that, I should, too.

Violet was always a little bit more timid and quiet so I guess it's only natural that it didn't even occur to Mom that she would be dating.

"I'm not sure where you're getting at with all of this. What does it matter?" Mom asks, holding herself by grasping onto her shoulders.

I sympathize.

The thing about investigating a missing person case is that you have to get into that person's background. You have to dig up old wounds.

You have to ask questions that the families may not always want answers to and in this case I can tell that my mom is uncomfortable.

I look at the steering wheel and all of the dust that has collected between the windshield and the dashboard. I know that I have to tell her the truth.

"I will tell you something, but only if you promise to keep it between us, because Natalie's parents can't know. The person who told me this told me this in confidence."

Mom nods.

"There's a possibility that she and Natalie were a couple. Well, maybe not a couple, but romantically involved."

"Who said this?"

"I can't tell you that."

"Well, how do you know if that's a reliable source and not just someone spreading lies?"

I take a deep breath and finally admit, "I saw a video, Mom. They made a video of themselves kissing."

"They did?"

"Yeah."

"It wasn't just pretend?"

"No, it wasn't. It was a real recording."

"Why would they do that?"

"They're young and stupid and like everyone else, they like to record themselves doing everything."

"So, she and Natalie were kissing?"

I nod.

"And why does that matter?" Mom asks.

"It might mean that she and Natalie ran away. Natalie's parents were very strict. They would have not taken this seriously. They would not have taken this lightly. They couldn't handle something like that. I mean, it means ... I have no idea what it means. That's why I'm asking *you* about it."

Mom swallows hard, looks at me again, and admits, "She never mentioned it to me, but I wish she had."

There's a faraway glance in her eyes. She looks distant and tired, but not angry, not in the least.

I had no idea how my mom would react to this news. Unlike Natalie's mother, she didn't have firm, strict opinions that she had vocalized.

At the same time, there are so many things that she disapproves of, especially things that I used to do, that I was pretty sure she would disapprove of this.

"Why are you acting like this?" Mom asks. "Why are you acting like this is some difficult thing for you to ask me about?"

"Well, frankly, I have no idea where you stand on people being gay."

"Please, don't insult me. Where I stand on that? People are gay. There's nowhere to stand."

"I just remember how you were when I was a kid," I start to say but she interrupts me.

"Things were very different when you were growing up, Kaitlyn. I can't believe that you would even compare the two," Mom says. "If Violet has feelings for Natalie and they want to explore those feelings, that's one thing. What you were doing was rebelling. You were hooking up with guys and you were trying to find something that you could not find by acting like that. You were trying to get approval. You were trying to fight back against me.

That's what I wanted you to stop doing. It's not about being sexually active or exploring your feelings for other people. It's about not trying to get back at your parents by doing something with your body. That's what I was upset with."

I'm tempted to bring up the money she borrowed from me to pay the mortgage, but I decide to keep my mouth shut.

16

_____

When I get back to LA, my thoughts keep going back to what my mom said about Violet and me. I know that Violet is young and I don't want to think of her as gone forever, but it makes me sad to know that the person that she is will be forever altered by whatever it is that happened to her.

Unless she did run away with Natalie.

My mom and I never talked about the teenager that I used to be. She would mention it only in passing, but that was about it.

Talking to her about Violet and that kiss, I realized that my mom wasn't at all the person that I thought that she was. There's still so much that I don't know about her, but I wonder if it's like that for everyone.

Your parents are kind of a mystery to you, even if you're close. You live in the same house, but because of all the time that separates you, you go through these phases in your relationship.

In the beginning, they're gods and goddesses, maybe a tyrant if you get a bad one, but mostly, they are rulers of your universe.

As years pass, you stand up to that.

You start to find your voice.

You start to challenge them and you separate.

You create your own identity, in opposition to theirs or maybe along with it, if you get along.

Are there people that really even understand their parents?

Are there parents that really understand their children?

I don't know. I only know about the parents that I had and they have always been somewhat of an enigma.

When I get back to the precinct, I get a text message that they've tracked down the kid who withdrew the money from the ATM.

I down a cup of coffee, use the restroom, and head straight to the interrogation room. The kid's name is Kenny Tuffin.

He's barely sixteen and has long, scraggly hair, loose-fitting clothing, and a skateboard that's practically attached to his arm.

I'm waiting for him outside the interrogation room. His mother had given us permission to interview him without her presence and that kind of confidence can be misleading.

Kenny's hair falls into his eyes, and his shoulders are sloped down, making him look tired and completely turned inward.

"Thanks for coming in," I say, after I introduce myself and open the folder demonstratively in front of him.

I already know as much as I can about the Janine Sato case.

My main concern is how does Kenny know Nick, the guy in whose apartment Janine's body was found?

Nick is still nowhere to be found and Peter Millian, his father, is no longer being as talkative and cooperative as he was originally.

I assume that it's dawning on him that there may be a chance that his son, a US Marine, might have had something to do with this.

"Can I offer you something to drink or eat?" I ask.

Kenny shakes his head no.

"Okay, well, let's get right to it. What can you tell me about that money that you withdrew out of the ATM?" I show him the photos from the security camera and it looks like it's physically painful for him to look at them.

"That's you, right?" I ask, even though we have already positively ID'd him as the person on the tape.

"I don't know what this has anything to do with," Kenny says. "I didn't steal that money."

"This isn't about that."

"What do you mean? You're a detective, right?" He leans over and puts his elbows on the table with his face so

close to mine I see how badly it has been sc
acne.

"So, you didn't get the money from the ATM

"No, I did," he admits it, "but I didn't keep it.'

"Oh, yeah? What happened to it?"

"Listen, I knew that this was a bad idea and I shouldn't have done it, but I can't really snitch on the guy."

"So, it's a guy," I say, keeping his gaze with my eyes for as long as he can handle it.

He looks away first.

Kenny looks scared and lost, so I wonder if it's better to put some pressure on him or act more like a friend. It's hard to know which decision is best, but I decide to go the softer route at first.

I can always go harder later.

"Kenny, you need to tell me what happened. Someone has been murdered."

"What?" His mouth drops open and his eyes get big like two quarters. "I had nothing to do with that. You have to believe me."

"I do, but I need your help. I need you to tell me what happened. Why did you get that money?"

"There's this guy, Danny Usoro. He works for my dad's landscaping company. He asked me to withdraw the money. He said that he couldn't do it himself."

"Why?" I ask.

don't know. I asked him, but none of the reasons made any sense."

"So you did it for him?"

"Yeah. He paid me with pizza."

"You withdrew $400 at a time?"

"Yep, at three different ATMs."

"How much pizza did you get in return?"

"Four boxes," he says.

I ask him more about the details of the transaction, knowing that somewhere in the other room, my fellow investigators are already trying to find out who Danny Usoro is and get in contact with him.

"You said that he works for your dad's landscaping company? What does he do exactly?"

"Um, just whatever. He kind of does it on the side."

"On the side from what?"

"He plays in a band, so they have gigs in West Hollywood and up in the Valley. He does landscaping in his spare time."

"Okay, okay. Thank you for your help."

"You can't tell him that I told you," Kenny says, giving me the most innocent look that I've seen in a while. "He'll be really mad at me."

"You did nothing wrong, okay? Why don't you stay here and I'll get your statement on record? I'll be right back."

I walk out of the room, surprised by how quickly that conversation happened.

"Did he say that the guy who paid him in pizza to get the money out of the ATM is named Danny Usoro?" Captain asks.

I nod.

"I thought that name sounded familiar. I was looking through the interviews of the names of the neighbors."

I nod.

It's standard procedure to canvas the neighborhood and ask everyone, especially everyone in the building, what they might have heard or seen and where they were.

"Well, there's a Daniel Usoro listed as one of Nick's neighbors. You think that's a coincidence?"

I raise an eyebrow.

After getting Kenny Tuffin's statement into written form and having him sign it, I head over to Danny Usoro's apartment.

17

When I arrive at his apartment building, it's mid-morning and the black and yellow police tape is still wrapped around Nick's door.

From the looks of it, no one has taken it off or entered through the front door. Danny Usoro lives two apartments down. I knock softly at first on the peeling paint, but it's not until I slam the knocker that I finally hear some movement inside.

He staggers to the door, his feet are heavy on the parquet floor and he opens the door, leaving just a crack.

His hair, thick and slightly curly, stands up on end. His face has creases on it from the pillow and his eyes are bloodshot.

I introduce myself and show him my badge. He opens the door a little bit further but doesn't invite me inside.

He's wearing a loose pair of flannel pants with a drawstring and no shirt. He has a muscular, broad shouldered body, pale, and covered in tattoos. There's a big black spider on his left pectoral muscle and something that looks like medieval armor plate around his left shoulder.

"I have a few questions about what happened in Nick's apartment. Would you mind if I came in?" I ask, tilting my head to the side.

I want to appear as approachable as possible and it seems to work.

The apartment is a standard one bedroom with a living room that starts right at the front door. The walls inside have recently been painted and there are movie posters all over them: *Scarface, Pulp Fiction, The Boondock Saints,* and then a surprise one, *Cider House Rules.*

The last one is a poignant historical drama based on a book by John Irving about an orphan who apprentices for a doctor specializing in abortions. He has mixed feelings about it and falls in love with a woman who gets one.

"*Cider House Rules?*" I ask, pointing to the poster. "That seems like an unusual choice."

"Yes. You'd know that given the fact that we've met only a few minutes before?" Danny points out, crossing his arms.

"Sorry, I didn't mean anything by it."

"Yeah, right," he says and walks over to the refrigerator, pouring himself a glass of water without offering me anything. "That was my mom's favorite movie, okay? Is that what you came here to talk to me about? What movies I like to watch?"

"No, not at all."

Danny walks over to the couch, sits down, and nudges for me to do the same.

Blue light streams through the windows. The blinds are up and there are no curtains to filter it.

I feel like we got off on a bad foot, but I try to suck it up and just move forward.

"Can you tell me anything that you know about Nick?" I ask.

"I already told all of this to this other cop in a uniform who was here."

"Yes, but it's important we go over the story a few times, just in case."

"In case what? In case you catch me in a lie?"

He's abrasive, sitting forward on the couch in an intimidating manner. He doesn't intimidate me, but he's clearly trying to tell me that he's not worried about a thing.

I open my notebook and take out a pen. I've noticed that this gesture alone seems to put people at ease.

They're not just having a conversation with me, they are having a conversation with someone who is writing down their observations and answers.

"Nick is my neighbor. I saw him around the building and talked to him a few times. He was a cool cat."

"Were you guys friends?"

"No. I just went to a party he had briefly, but that's about it."

"What is it that you do, Danny?"

He points to the pirate ship across his stomach.

I furrow my brow and ask, "Tattoos?"

"Yeah. I work in a tattoo shop down on Melrose. I work for a landscaping business part time while I try to get my rock band off the ground."

"You're in a rock band?" I ask as if this is a surprise to me.

"*Broken Pirates*," he says, pointing to the 17th century ship with four masts on his stomach. "We play at *Whisky a Go-Go* and a few other spots, putting together our first record."

"Congratulations," I say. "What landscaping business do you work at?"

"Tuffin."

"How many hours a week?"

"Probably twenty, sometimes thirty. It varies. I mainly do businesses around here, West Hollywood, that kind of thing."

I nod.

"Hey, you should come see us play some time," he says, leaning over.

Talking about his band seems to have put him in a better frame of mind. He winks at me and smiles.

"Are you flirting with me?" I ask.

"No, of course not. I'd never flirt with a cop."

"You wouldn't, huh?" I ask, sitting back against the couch.

"You seem like the type of girl who likes to have a good time. I don't see a ring. You like rock music?"

"Yes, I do," I say, hating the fact that I'm enjoying the moment.

I tell myself not to flirt back, but it's a little difficult because Danny Usoro is quite easy on the eyes.

His are almond shaped and a color of deep green, even though they're a little puffy and swollen from probably a little bit too much booze.

His face is angular and he has a strong jawline. He knows exactly how to hold his head and lean over to make a girl feel special.

"Listen, you should come to one of our shows." He hands me his card.

It has the band's logo, website, and his phone number on it.

"Your rock band has a business card?" I ask. "Isn't that a little bit traditional? Corporate?"

"Listen, we're going to make it big. Making contacts is the way to do it, especially in this business. If you go on our website, you'll be able to see where we're playing. You should come out on Friday."

"Nope, I can't." I shake my head.

"You're doing something important?"

"Yes. Investigating a murder."

"Oh, come on. Don't be like that," he says, smiling with his dimples coming through.

"Man, he is one smooth guy," I say to myself.

It would be a shame if he had something to do with this and suddenly, I regret even thinking that.

"What can you tell me about Nick?" I ask, trying to focus my attention back to what I'm here for.

"I don't know, nothing really."

"Have you met the girl who was found murdered in his apartment?"

"No. Janine, was that her name?"

"Yeah. You never met her? You never saw her?"

"No. I mean, I saw pictures of her that the deputy showed me, but no, I've never seen her before. Were they together?"

"That's what I'm trying to find out."

"That's too bad. He seemed like a quiet guy, but you know how it is sometimes with quiet guys."

"How is it?" I ask.

"Still waters run deep, isn't that how the saying goes?"

I nod, not entirely sure how to take this conversation.

On one hand, he's being open and sharing, but on the other, I feel like something is going on below the surface.

"He did get a tattoo at my girlfriend's, actually my fiancée's, shop."

"Oh, what kind of tattoo?"

"Not sure. He had a few, he got a few crappy ones when he was in the Marines, but she did a big one for him. I can't remember."

"Who is your fiancée?"

"Eve Navarro. She works on Melrose."

"She's a tattoo artist?"

"Yep. She's been doing it for about five years now. She was working there for a couple when she moved out from Oklahoma."

"Oh, wow. Okay. Can you write me her phone number and the address here?" I hand him my pen.

After he hands me back the notebook, he says, "You know, I was hitting on you earlier, but I don't want you to think that I'm some sort of cheating ass or something."

"Yeah, of course not," I say sarcastically.

"You know what I mean."

"So why did you flirt if you have a fiancée?" I say, getting up and heading toward the door.

"We both like to party. It's an open relationship."

"You both date people on the side?"

"No, we date people at the same time and you're just her type."

I walk out of the interview feeling a little bit less steady on my feet. It's not that I've never been hit on by someone I questioned before; it's just that Danny Usoro definitely has a way with words.

It helps that he's quite easy on the eyes with his caramel skin and all of those nicely placed tattoos add to the overall aura of the type of persona that he wants to project.

Before heading back to the office, I realize I forgot my iPad at home and stop by to grab it.

The interview went a little bit smoother and faster than I thought it would so I have some time to spare, a good forty-five minutes that I can take off from work.

I decide that if I'm going to be home and I'm going to relax, I'm going to do it all the way. When I get home, I strip off my work clothes, including the tight bra that pinches right underneath my breasts, change into a loose fitting flannel shirt and my favorite pair of oversized pjs. I make myself a cup of coffee, put my hair up in a loose ponytail, and savor the moment.

I don't have much time off in this job and I've learned to take advantage of every few minutes that I can. Taking off the bra and changing into comfortable clothes is just part of that process.

It takes very little time, but it goes a long way to putting me into that deep state of relaxation. I go to Prime video and start an old episode of *Disappeared* on the Investigative Network.

I've seen a number of these and they usually profile people who have gone missing under suspicious circumstances. Bodies have never been found, and in some cases, it's not even clear whether they're gone at all or maybe left on their own volition.

There are a number of seasons of this show and I've never watched it much until one night when I was feeling frustrated and completely alone, trying to process what happened to Violet.

The show brought me a little bit of peace.

It made me realize that I'm not the only one going through all of this. Sometimes it's good to have company when you're in misery.

You forget that you're not the only one in the world going through something hard and that makes it better, in some sick perverse way. Since the show has been on the air for quite some time, I always make it a point to check at the end of the episode whether the person is still missing or not.

Most of the time they are still missing. On occasion, however, a body is found years later, and a few times, the person was found alive, living a new life in another part of the world.

The scratching of keys in the door break my concentration.

When I turn around, I see Sydney.

18

"Hey, what are you doing here?" we ask each other almost simultaneously and then laugh.

"I had some time before I had to get back," I say, "so I wanted to have some breakfast and just relax. You?"

"Just stopping by to get something."

She's dressed in jeans and a t-shirt, with her hair pulled up in a high braid, tied with a ribbon.

Her makeup is flawless, but I notice that there's a little bit too much concealer under her eyes and she always tries to look a little bit more put-together when things are particularly tough.

"How's everything? How are you doing? Sorry I haven't been around."

"No worries." She grabs a glass, pours some water in, and plops down on the couch next to me.

The sun is streaming in through the open window, creating a halo-like effect around her head.

We chitchat about nothing in particular. She dances around asking about Violet and I avoid asking about her breakup.

It's hard to figure out when someone wants to talk about it, when you should be there for them, and when it's best to draw their attention elsewhere to provide some comic relief.

Eventually, I catch her up on what happened in Big Bear.

"They're going to find her," Sydney promises me, but she has the same expression on her face that we all do when we make those promises to the families.

There's no way that she can know that and that means that it's really something of an empty promise, but I appreciate it anyway.

"What's going on with Patrick? Have you officially broken up?"

"Well, that's kind of the thing," she says, hesitating.

I wait for her to continue. She licks her lips and looks down at her nails that are filed into sharp points and painted a muted color of forest green.

"I think we're going to get back together."

My mouth nearly drops open.

I turn my body to face her, leaning over, but before I can say anything, she says, "Listen, I know that it's stupid, but I have to give him another chance."

"Why?"

"He said he was sorry."

"Please don't tell me that you love him."

"I do love him."

"I know that you do. Otherwise, you wouldn't even be thinking this insane thing."

"It's not insane. We have a really good connection."

"What about what he did? What about all of that stuff that you found on his phone? Is that okay with you? If he's going to do that to you now, what's he going to do after you've been together for a few years or a few decades?"

"Listen, I didn't come here to have you judge me."

That's when I know.

When she uses that word 'judge,' that's when I know that her mind is made up.

She's not going to back away from this and if I keep pushing her harder or if I keep trying to make her agree with me, then we might not be friends after all.

After all, it's not my place to say who she is supposed to be with. It's for her to decide.

"Listen, I'm sorry about that. I didn't want to come off being so judgmental or anything like that. I'm just worried about you."

"Yeah, I know and I'm worried about it, too, but I have to give it a chance."

"Why?" The word slips out before I can stop myself.

"We're going to have a baby."

I sit here, stunned and staring at her.

Sydney is going to have a baby.

My Sydney.

My friend.

It's something that happens all the time to people everywhere, because if it didn't, we wouldn't have much of a species.

Still, it feels so odd, foreign, and almost unnatural for *Sydney Sutka* to be pregnant.

"Congratulations," I say, forcing myself to smile and to give her a hug.

"I wasn't happy at first. I mean, things are so complicated with Patrick, but we were already engaged and I do love him. He promised that he would never do that again."

I nod.

Hasn't this story played out a million times before to millions and millions of other women?

How does it work out?

Not that well, but we keep trying anyway.

I'm not saying that it's a certainty that Patrick would cheat. It's not.

Every person is unique, different.

But if this is what he will do when you are just dating and are supposed to be in your honeymoon period, what's going to happen when there are actual pressures of children, work, etc?

How's he going to cope with a wife that asks him to stop spending every weekend on the golf course?

I don't know.

Maybe Patrick Flannery will be that one beacon of hope.

I'm sure that there were others that have made mistakes and then never cheated again, but all I have is his past behavior to judge him on.

"I know that you're mad at him. I know that you're angry for what he did, but please don't be," Sydney says.

A rogue tear breaks free and rolls down her cheek.

I exhale slowly and I look up at her. I try to think of something nice to say, something encouraging.

"I always thought that you two made a good couple," I say.

This *isn't* a lie.

"But?" she asks.

"There is no 'but.'"

"So, you think this is okay?"

"No." I shake my head.

"Kaitlyn, come on."

"I'm going to be here for you, your child, and your husband because I want to be your friend, but... "

"But what?"

I would never do that to myself.

I would run away from him.

I would raise a child on my own.

I would have visitation, but I wouldn't let that man back into my personal life.

"We all make different decisions," I finally say, keeping the rest of it to myself.

She leans over and gives me a hug. I wrap my hands tightly around her shoulders and tell her that it's going to be okay.

She begins to cry and I hold her as she sobs.

"I don't want anyone to know about what he did," she whispers over and over again.

I promise her that I won't tell a soul and I feel sorry for the fact that I think I might be in this position, consoling her over what her spouse did for many years to come.

When Sydney finally pulls away, I decide not to push her any further.

I'm going to support her. I don't want to ruin my friendship over this because I've lost friendships to not liking boyfriends before.

Who she dates and marries is not my call. It's hers.

It's my job to just be there, no matter how much I disagree.

"Will you come to my OBGYN appointment tomorrow?" Sydney asks, wiping the last of her tears off her cheeks.

"Me?" I ask, surprised.

"Patrick can't make it. He's working a long shift."

I promise to be there.

fter getting dressed and putting everything back into my satchel bag, I drive over to Eve Navarro's tattoo shop.

Online it said that it opens at eleven a.m.. and I'm here a little bit after. The elderly gentleman with tattoos going up his neck and face tells me that she's in the back and calls her over. I stand up front looking through the big binder of tattoo designs.

Just as I lose myself in an intricate back tattoo of an underwater scene that looks like it could be the real thing, a pretty girl with large, dark eyes wearing jeans and boots comes out to shake my hand.

She has a flannel shirt tied around her waist and a few geometric style black and white tattoos on her upper arms.

I introduce myself and she seems to know everything that I have to say.

"I've been kind of expecting you," she says. "Danny told me that you'd be stopping by. I just wasn't sure when or that you would look like this."

"Like what?" I ask.

"I don't know. Like you're my age and a detective. That's pretty impressive."

"Yeah, I guess." I shrug. "I'm not an artist like you though."

She gives me a smile out of the corner of her lips.

"Can we talk somewhere private?" I ask.

She nods and takes me in the back. The room isn't exactly private in that it has a door, but it's secluded enough and the gentleman whom I've met earlier is nowhere around.

Eve Navarro has long blonde hair, no doubt extensions, thick fake lashes, lips filled with filler and looks like she walked out of a magazine.

Dressed in a push-up bra that makes her breasts look like they're practically touching her chin, she knows exactly how to move her body to look both seductive and approachable.

"Do you have any tattoos?" she asks. "Detective Carr?"

"No, I don't."

"Never wanted one?"

"Uh, I wouldn't say that, but..."

"But what?"

"I don't know. I sometimes think back to the tattoos that I would have gotten if I got one when I was twenty and I don't know if I'd want to have that on my body anymore."

"Yeah, I guess. We can't really think of it that way."

"What do you mean?" I ask.

"Well, yes, they're permanent but only in that they're drawing on your skin. But really, they're a representation of the person that you once were and that's not exactly a permanent thing. If it's done badly, I understand why people may not want it anymore. If it's of an ex-boyfriend or an ex-husband, names are never a good idea."

She laughs, tossing her hair.

"If they are of objects and symbols of something that you used to love that maybe you don't anymore, well, that's just how life is, isn't it?" Eve continues. "Sometimes, you grow more mature. Your interests change, but that doesn't mean that the tattoo is no longer relevant. It's a mark of the passage of time."

"I like that," I say. "You have a beautiful way of thinking about it."

"Well, I do think about them for at least ten hours a day," she says, raising her eyebrow.

She crosses her hands across her chest, making her breasts even more pronounced and that's when I see a small minimalist style one of just a few lines, a perfect circle, and a couple of dots, splashed with watercolor right at the collarbone of her neck.

"Wow. That one's really good," I say, pointing it out.

"Watercolors have become my specialty. Small minimalist tattoos. Also, they require a lot of precision. The simpler the tattoo, the less places there is to hide your deficiencies as an artist."

"The circle is perfect," I say.

"I didn't do this one, but my colleague did. You can't go back over circles or you shouldn't more than once. The lines get too dark and in designs like this, they have to be just right."

I nod in agreement as if I know anything about the subject matter.

I'm about to sit down on the chair where the client sits to get the tattoo, but she pulls out another chair from behind the desk.

She sits on the swivel stool, dropping her arms to her sides.

"So, what can I help you with?"

I ask her about Nick. I need her to tell me anything and everything that she knows about him.

"I met him a few times when Danny had a party. I think I went to one of his parties as well. They were neighbors, but they weren't close. I had a beer with him and asked him about being in the Marines. He didn't want to talk about it. I got the sense that he killed a few people."

That statement comes out of nowhere and takes me by surprise. I actually haven't done much research into Nick's background besides the fact that he served in the military. It did occur to me that he could be suffering from PTSD from what happened while he was in the service.

"What did you guys talk about, specifically?" I ask, pulling out my notebook and jotting down a few notes.

"He said that he lost a close friend. He showed me his dog tags. He wore them around his neck."

"Wow. Just like that? He told you about him?"

"We had a few beers. I got the sense that he wanted to sleep with me even though he never really tried to ask me out. He knew I was Danny's girlfriend, but we were flirting and drinking a little bit too much," Eve says, tossing her hair from one shoulder to the other.

"I asked him about what it was like. He said it was shitty," she continues. "He said he was sick of it. He was sick of people dying and he was sick of killing people. He said that there has to be more to life than that."

She nervously spins on the stool, keeping her feet on the floor.

"Do you know what happened to his friend?" I ask. "Like his name?"

She puts her chin up in the air and crosses her arms, supporting her head with one palm. Rolling over to the desk, she grabs a fresh page in the sketch pad, and starts to draw something.

I get up to see and see an outline of a dog tag, followed by some shading and a name.

She pauses for a moment when she finishes the W on Matthew, then makes an A with a period after, and Hoag.

"That's right. Hoag," she says, racing her index finger in the air. "I couldn't remember and sketching what I saw helps a lot."

"Can I keep this?" I ask.

"Of course."

"Can you tell me what happened to Matthew Hoag?"

20

Eve props her head up with her hand, leaning over the table. I repeat my question and her eyes refuse to meet mine.

"He got blown up in a Humvee," she finally says.

"What?" I lean closer.

"Nick was supposed to go and then he got called back for something and Matt went in his place. The car got blown up and everyone got really hurt, but Matt was killed on impact," she says with a sigh. "When Nick told me about it, he said that it didn't feel like life was worth living after that, like he had gotten his friend killed, but he also couldn't kill himself because that would mean that his friend died for nothing. He said he was living in purgatory."

"Purgatory?" I repeat her word.

"Yes." Eve nods. "He said that he was in a waiting room, just living life that he didn't want to live, waiting to die

but not really. It was really deep and I fe
for him. I asked him if maybe he shoul
someone."

"Like a therapist?" I ask.

"It can be really helpful. I go once a week and ever since
I started, all of my relationships and everything have
really improved. It helps me make sense of the world and
it helps me process my feelings. We don't have enough
opportunities of that in real life. Everyone is just judging
us, you know?"

"Yeah," I say, realizing just how much I agree with her.

"Do you see a therapist?" Eve asks.

"I have before but mainly when I had to."

"I'm actually thinking about going to school for it."

"You are?" I ask. "What about this?"

"I don't know. I like it, but the clients are a little too
much, too demanding. A lot of people want designs that
they find online that other artists have done. They don't
want to let me do what I want to do, which makes sense
because it's their body, but it makes for a difficult
situation. I'm not a tracer. I'm an artist."

"I'd encourage you to do whatever you want," I say. "Life
is too short to not pursue your passions."

"What about *you*?" Eve asks, raising an eyebrow.

I clench my jaw.

I don't know how this conversation's gotten away from
me so much. On one hand, I want to make her feel
comfortable enough to open up and tell me things that

, she wouldn't otherwise. On the other hand, the versation has suddenly turned personal.

"Did you always want to be a police officer?" she asks, choosing her words carefully.

"I've always wanted to be a detective," I say.

I look down at my notepad and tell her that we've gotten a little bit off track.

"Can you tell me more about Nick? He said that he felt like he was in purgatory. Do you think that he could have been violent?"

"No," she says quickly, "there was a fight that broke out at one of the parties and he broke it up. He didn't instigate anything. He didn't seem like the type of guy who was out looking for trouble."

"Were the parties the only times you talked to him?" I ask.

"No. He actually also came here. I gave him a tattoo."

"You did?" I ask.

"Yeah. Statue of Liberty kind of on the side of his stomach. He had a big scar there and when I asked him what it was, he said he didn't want to talk about it, so I assumed that it had something to do with being in the Middle East."

"How did it turn out?"

"He loved it. I made it very detailed. He wanted it to be very realistic. It wasn't his first one. He had a few others done on a base somewhere, but they weren't that great and he seemed to be impressed with mine when he left. He gave me a big tip."

I tap my pen on my notebook.

"What about Janine Sato?"

"She was the one who was murdered?" Eve asks, lowering her voice to a whisper.

"Have you ever met her?"

"No."

"Do you know if they were together?"

"No, I don't think so, but I don't know."

I show her a picture of Janine on my phone to jog her memory.

"Oh, wait. This is Janine?"

I nod.

"Actually, yeah. I saw her at a party at Danny's, but I didn't talk to her and she didn't have any tattoos."

"No, she didn't," I say.

I'm about to ask her some more questions when the man that led me into the shop comes in and pulls her away, telling her about a walk-in client.

"I'm sorry, but I have to take this," she says.

"I have enough for now, but I'll be in touch if I have any other questions."

"Yeah, of course," she says. "Call me anytime."

As I head toward the door, Eve runs up to me.

"One more thing. I really don't think that Nick had anything to do with that girl's murder."

"You don't?" I ask. "Any particular reason?"

"No, but I just really don't think that he did. He seemed so quiet, shy, and not in that, 'I'm quiet, shy, and secretly a serial killer.' No. Not at all. He didn't give me any creepy vibes. He wasn't intense. He was just like this big teddy bear. He just seemed lost more than anything. I really wish that he had talked to someone about all that guilt that he felt."

"So, what *do* you think happened?" I ask. "If he didn't kill her, how did she end up dead in his apartment and why is he gone?"

"I have no idea. Maybe somebody else did it, trying to frame him?"

I grab my purse.

"But it seems unlikely," Eve adds and I couldn't agree more.

21

A ll the way on the drive over to the precinct, I review the interview with Eve Navarro. In my mind, I go over everything that she said and although it has a lot of interesting highlights, one stands out.

She said that her boyfriend, Danny Usoro, had met the murder victim, Janine Sato, either at one of the parties that he hosted or one of Nick's parties.

This stands in stark contrast to what Danny told me earlier. Danny had insisted that he had never met Janine, probably to not place himself as someone who could possibly know anything about what happened, but now there's a contradiction.

There's no point for Eve to lie, but there is a reason for Danny. The question now is what do I do with this information?

Later that afternoon, we arrange to have Danny brought in for more of an official interview, this time at the precinct. It will be recorded and I will be the one asking him questions.

He volunteers to come and he does not mention bringing a lawyer, which is good news. Lawyers are a constitutional right, but they're not great news for us. They ask questions, they stop us from asking more, and they get their clients to shut up.

Of course, false confessions are relatively common, a lot more than you'd even expect. The people who are particularly vulnerable to giving untrue testimony are those suffering from mental illness or mental handicaps. As far as I know, Danny suffers from neither.

He's here to clear up a few confusing points and contradictions, and hopefully give us more information about what he knows.

"Carr," Captain Medvil calls my name as I walk past his office.

Holding a Big Gulp of Coke in one hand and a mug of coffee in the other hand, he gestures for me to come in.

"I'm putting Thomas Abrams on the interrogator list," he says and cold sweat runs down my spine.

"No. I can do this by myself."

"It will be better if you work together. Good cop, bad cop, you know, that kind of thing. This is going to require a delicate balance."

"You don't think that I can be delicate enough?"

"That's not what I said."

Medvil spills some coffee on his hand and winces in pain, sucking it up into his mouth. He grabs a few napkins and wipes his pants.

"Why do they always make it so hot?" he complains and I give him a few seconds to calm down before arguing my case against Thomas Abrams.

"As an interrogator, he can be quite rushed. He can intimidate suspects too much. It will be easier for me to work on this by myself."

"I know that it will be *easier* for you," Captain Medvil says, sitting down behind his cluttered desk.

There are piles of folders everywhere, even blocking part of the computer.

"This decision is not about making *your* life easier. This is about what's good for the case."

I'm about to argue against him again, but he raises his hand up and tells me to go.

I walk out defeated and full of anger. The captain has no right to put Thomas Abrams on this case. I can do this by myself. He hasn't worked it at all from the beginning, so why would he be on it now?

"Hey there." Thomas waves hello to me and gets up from the chair right across from my desk.

He has heard the news and he's here waiting to prepare.

The interview starts in forty-five minutes. I force a smile on my face. I don't want him to know how annoyed I am, frustrated, or that I have any feelings about this whatsoever.

Since the last time I saw him, Thomas has gotten rid of that standard issue cop haircut of having it short all around, almost bordering on a buzz cut, and grown the top of his hair a little longer. The sides fall into a fade.

His hair is the color of wheat with just a few highlights and it has just enough product to not make it look like it's soggy wet.

His eyes are hazel and his narrow nose, somewhat delicate cheekbones, and jaw make him look beautiful and remind me of why I fell for him in the first place.

"I guess you heard the good news," he says and I hold the folder in front of me even tighter, trying to keep my face perfectly still and relaxed to not show any weakness. "Sorry. I had no idea that Captain Medvil was going to assign me to this."

I don't believe him.

In fact, I wouldn't be surprised if he had asked for this case in the first place, but I let it slide.

"Yeah, sure, whatever."

I sit down in my chair and open the folder.

"I caught up on it last night. Now you talked to Eve Navarro today, right? What did she say?"

"Shit," I say to myself silently.

Last night, Medvil assigned Thomas to this case and he didn't even tell me until now.

Why the hell not? I guess because he didn't want me to argue with him for a day, or maybe... I pause for a moment while I think.

It suddenly occurs to me. Medvil has no idea that we were ever together.

Typically, police officers who become romantically involved have to file special paperwork with human resources. We never did.

Right before we were going to file and make it official with the department, I found out the truth about him.

I haven't told that many people and the two people that do know have promised to keep it a secret. It seemed that Thomas didn't tell many people either, especially since it doesn't make him look too good after what happened with our breakup.

"Listen, let's just be professional here," Thomas says. "Tell me what Eve Navarro said."

I furrow my brows.

By saying let's be professional, he is implying that I am being unprofessional, which couldn't be further from the truth.

He's just trying to get a rise out of me.

"First of all, I'm perfectly fine with you working with me on this," I lie.

He smiles at me in that casual way almost like he's humoring me.

"Eve made it seem like there were a number of parties that both Nick and Danny had at their apartments and that both were invited to each. She never met-"

"So, what do you think it means?" he asks.

"Probably means that Danny's hiding something."

"Like what?"

"Maybe he knows where Nick is now. When I first talked to him, he made it seem like he didn't really know him very well," I say. "They were neighbors. They saw each other occasionally, but that was it. After talking to Eve, I get the sense that their situation could be a little bit closer. They were acquaintances. They've definitely partied together. I mean, Eve had talked to Danny quite a bit. He seemed to have opened up to her. He told her about his friend who got killed and that how responsible he felt."

I open my notepad and go through more details from Eve.

We discuss the strategy, which isn't really a strategy because we don't really know what we're going to do and how we're going to schedule this questioning until we start talking to him.

This is where interrogation becomes more of an art form. You ask the wrong questions at the wrong time and the person's not going to come forward and is not going to tell you what you want to hear.

I don't know if Eve would have told Thomas everything that she told me.

We made a connection.

She felt like she could trust me and that's what it's all about.

However, when the person comes in for an interview at the precinct, they're more on guard. They're nervous. It's an official environment and is harder to get people to open up.

With some who are on the periphery involved with the crime, you can use the weight of the department to push them over the edge and to scare them into telling you the truth.

But it's harder to do that with people who are involved. They don't want to implicate themselves.

They don't want to put themselves where they could be accused of being guilty of something, but they do want to explain.

They want to draw attention elsewhere.

I'm not saying that Danny's a suspect. He's anything but that. The main suspect here is Nick, but my suspicion is that Danny is helping him.

"The way we handle Danny is going to either lead us toward Nick or away from him," I say.

"Couldn't agree more," Thomas says with a smile, taking me by surprise.

"Listen, I've always thought that you were a good cop. That was never our problem."

22

I clench my jaw and I see him see me do this. I hate how vulnerable he makes me feel.

Just with a few lines of dialogue and suddenly I feel like I'm falling apart, even though on the surface I'm not.

I don't know if he can read all of my signs. Probably not.

I would say that most people can't and most people don't even notice all these little twitches, all of these little facial tics and auras that they put out into the world, which I pick up on.

I can feel the way other people are feeling. At work, it feels like a superpower, but growing up it was more like a burden.

It has always been something of a gift of mine. Whenever anyone felt awkward or uncomfortable, I felt it. I sympathized and I empathized, but I couldn't get that feeling off of me.

As I grew up, I learned how to deal with it better.

I learned to accept it and eventually deflect it. Now, there's almost like this thin shield of plexiglass separating me from the world. I can walk around with it and lift it up whenever I really need to make a connection.

That's what happened with Eve and that's what I hope will happen in this interrogation room with Danny.

I'm better at the informal interviews. There are comfortable seats, nice lighting, things to drink and munch on.

Here with the camera above our heads, it's hard to forget that you're at the police station. It's hard to forget that everything you're saying is being recorded and anyone who's ever seen at least one crime show knows that it's not a good idea to talk to the police.

"Our best bet," Thomas says, "is to make Danny feel involved, make him feel like he wants to tell us something to help find his friend."

"What if he is the one hiding him or helping him hide?" I ask.

"He probably is, but maybe this is his opportunity to draw our attention somewhere else or maybe he'll have some possible explanation for why Janine's body was found in his friend's apartment. If he has an explanation, there'll be more details to help us figure it all out."

Thomas is not telling me anything that I don't already know.

We're just brainstorming and coming up with an approach. I take a few big gulps of water before we walk to the interrogation room.

Danny is already waiting for us.

I take the lead with as casual of a manner as possible.

Thomas is an expert at this. Nothing is ever formal or precise, but it's meant to be that way. He comes off even a little bit stupid and that's what makes people think there's no way that he's going to figure anything out.

"Thanks for inviting me here, Detective Abrams," Danny says. "I'd really like to find my friend."

That's kind of a weird statement, but it's still early in the interrogation to start cataloging unusual comments.

"Why don't you call us Thomas and Kaitlyn?" I say.

I want him to think of us as his friends. I want to make him comfortable.

He nods approvingly and we get started from there.

Since Thomas is new here, he takes the liberty to ask Danny to go over the testimony that he had given me earlier to check it for any inconsistencies.

Most of the time the people we interview get a little annoyed when you ask them the same questions over and over again, but that's part of the job.

You have to make sure that the story stays the same and if it changes, it only changes slightly. We want to make sure that there aren't any glaring inconsistencies, but then again, if the story is exactly the same, verbatim, word for word, that's something to consider a little bit suspicious as well. Maybe in that case, someone memorized something instead of actually experiencing it.

As we talk to Danny, Thomas does a good job of playing my ignorant friend.

He acts like he doesn't know much about the case. He asks Danny to pose possible explanations for what could have happened. We act like we're here to ask him for his advice and for his help in figuring out who did it.

He is very helpful. He tells us a lot but nothing really specifically different. When I confront him about the fact that Eve mentioned that he was closer to Nick that he had led on, he just shrugs it off.

"What about Janine?" I ask. "Have you met her at one of those parties?"

"Yeah, maybe," he says.

"That's not what you said before."

"There were a lot of people there. Anything is possible."

We all know what he's trying to say. He's trying to give himself an out and give us what we want but not implicate himself too much.

After we review the case in general and Thomas develops a little bit of a rapport, we finally get to the point.

"Do you know a guy named Kenny Tuffin?" Thomas asks.

Danny's mouth drops open. Blood rushes away from his skin making it appear sallow and greenish.

"Kenny, who?" he asks, clearing his throat in the middle.

"Kenny Tuffin," Thomas says, leaning forward over the table. "You must know him."

"Yeah. Yeah. I kind of know him."

The wait for the next question is excruciating long and I kind of revel in it.

"Why did you ask Kenny to withdraw money from Nick's account for you?"

Danny leans back in his chair.

He didn't realize that we had gotten that much information and that realization is all over his face.

Little beads of sweat appear.

He starts to develop a nervous tic where he clinks his top teeth against the bottom and then tries to hide this fact.

"What are you talking about?" he asks.

"We found Kenny on camera withdrawing money," I say, talking slowly and taking in every single one of his expressions.

Each word feels like a gut punch.

The friendly happy-go-lucky guy practically disappears from one frame to another.

"When we talked to him about it, he said that he did it for you. He said he gave you $400 each from three ATMs and you paid him in pizza."

"Yeah, that happened," he admits it on camera and suddenly I'm happy that we're doing this interview here.

I say a silent prayer that he doesn't ask for legal counsel and instead tries to talk himself out of this situation.

"Nick gave me his card to use. I had lent him the money and he was giving it back to me."

"Why would he give you his card if he was going to disappear?" I ask.

"I don't know. Maybe he didn't have a plan, but he said that I could charge $1200 to it."

"If he let you use his card, why did you get Kenny to withdraw the money?" I ask, leaning back, feeling like I'm playing chess and winning, waiting for him to make the wrong move after he has already made five.

"Well, I knew that you were looking for him, so I didn't want to just charge the money to his card, but I needed it back for all the wedding expenses."

"Yeah, that makes sense," Thomas says in a way that makes it obvious that it doesn't.

"So, where is he now?"

"Who?"

"Nick." Thomas leans over the table in an intimidating fashion and waits.

"I have no idea. That part's totally true."

"What part is *not* true?" Thomas narrows his eyes.

"Look, I'm sorry I didn't tell you about the card. I just... I knew that you were looking for him."

"So you wanted to lead us on a wild goose chase trying to figure out who used the card?" I say, laying it all out on the table.

He nods but says nothing.

"If you know anything about Nick, you should tell us now. That would be the best way to protect him."

Danny shakes his head, swallows hard, looks down at the floor, and then back at me and Thomas.

He avoids my eyes and instead focuses on Thomas.

"I have no idea where Nick is now. I had no idea that he would do that."

"So you think that he did kill Janine?"

"I have no idea, but you did find her body there. So, in all likelihood, yes."

"If you're protecting him," I say, "it's going to be worse. You could be tried as an accessory."

He inhales quickly like taking in a gust of air, but then shakes his head, doubling down on his insistence that he has no idea where Nick is.

Neither of us believe him and I'm not so sure that he even believes himself, but for now, that's all that we can get out of him.

There's always that tension that if we push him too hard and it feels like he's being accused of something, then he'll ask for a lawyer.

We don't want that.

We want to press just hard enough to make him feel uncomfortable, to make some moves, maybe go home, make a call to his friend Nick, and tell him what happened.

That would be the ideal situation.

We let him go for now. We thank him for his time, shake his hand, and ask him to promise us to give us a call if he has any other information.

I leave him with the feeling like he has been helpful and that we believe what he's saying.

For now, that's good enough.

23

After interviewing Danny, Thomas and I step out and grab a cup of coffee. We're in the break room, a nondescript white kitchen with 70's style cabinets, a stainless steel refrigerator, and a Formica table top.

He opens the refrigerator, looks around, and then shuts it. If there's anything in there, it's labeled and therefore it doesn't belong to us.

I grab a bar from the vending machine.

I unwrap it and hold the porcelain mug of coffee that's hot, but nevertheless, slightly old, between my palms.

I lean over and tell him, "I wish we had talked to him more about the fact that he knew Janine."

Thomas nods.

"He was dodging the question. It was a big discrepancy. He lied about knowing her and who knows what else that could lead to."

"Listen, I get that as much as you do, but we're going to interview him again. We're going to push him on it, but I wanted to see what his reaction to Tuffin would be without him clamming up. I wanted him to feel like we're on his side."

He sits across from me, puts his face down in the coffee cup, and stares.

I'm not sure exactly where to go from here. I don't want to keep working with Thomas on this case and I need to figure out a way to get him off of it without telling Captain Medvil exactly *why* this isn't working.

"I think we make a pretty good team," Thomas says, giving me a little wink.

A little bit of his shirt is open at the top and I see part of his extensive tribal shoulder tattoo peeking out. It's unprofessional to show any of it at work and that's why he adjusts the fit of the collared shirt.

"No. I don't think we make a good team," I say, looking straight into his eyes. "I don't want any part of what I'm saying to be confusing or be misconstrued. I'm just working with you because you have been assigned, but this is *my* case. I can handle this on my own and I don't need your help."

"I'm not saying that you do," Thomas interrupts me. "Not at all. You're really competent and I know that you can do this all on your own. I'm just saying that isn't it nice to work on this like we used to back in the day?"

"No, it's not," I say without missing a beat.

"Oh, come on. Don't be like that," he jokes.

He's always been quite the smooth guy. He knows exactly what to say and how to say it.

That's why he's rarely wrong and even when he is in the wrong, he's not really the one doing anything improper, if you know what I mean.

I feel my jaw clench up and I realize that this is the last conversation that I want to be having right now.

It's one thing to talk about the case, but it's another to entertain this whole situation that I got myself into.

"What happened to the court reporter?" I say, leaning back in the chair.

Perhaps the best way to get him to shut up and stop reminiscing about all the good times we had is to think about all the bad ones.

"Nothing. Nothing happened to her. She's still around."

"Oh, yeah? When's the wedding?"

"We broke up."

This takes me by surprise.

"Really?"

"Yeah."

I should offer my condolences, but that would be too polite. We have been impolite for too long.

I caught him with her in bed. I moved out and we broke up, but our relationship was messed up long before he cheated on me.

It was then that I found out that she was pregnant.

I feel angry at myself by the fact that I heard rumors about the two of them and I believed everything that he had told me.

I get up to walk away.

I don't want to talk about this. It was hard enough to live through it.

"Look, I'm really sorry. I don't know if I've ever said that to you, but I am. I shouldn't have done any of-" Thomas says.

"You shouldn't have cheated on me or you shouldn't have lied?" I ask, unable to keep my composure.

The door to the kitchen creaks and my heart sinks. I've kept this a secret long enough, it would be monumentally stupid to expose myself now.

I walk out the other door and Thomas follows me, but I escape to Medvil's office. After a short debrief, Medvil instructs us to talk to the computer tech guy.

"I'm not sure how much of an update it is," he says, "but he's got something to tell you."

I check my phone and see that I'm CC'd on the email string.

This isn't the right time to bring up getting Thomas off the case.

Medvil is busy and distracted, especially since there's recently been an officer-involved shooting and the commissioner is pissed.

It's always unfortunate when an innocent bystander gets injured. In this case, the cop shot into the crowd, nicking him in the leg.

Medvil is pissed off. He has been fighting the commissioner to change certain practices of how things are done, but bureaucracy and police policies change slowly and the change has to come from the top. The captain has had numerous meetings with us to put in policies in place that would prevent future senseless shootings, but the commissioner is taking a hard line and nothing is going to change without it coming from the top.

"I can go talk to the tech by myself," I offer.

"No. I'd like to come," Thomas insists, knowing that we're going to have to walk all the way to the other side of the building and that's going to give us plenty of time to be alone.

I stop by my desk to grab my purse and excuse myself to go to the bathroom to gather my strength to put up with him for a little bit longer.

I give myself a brief pep talk. Thomas works in my department and that this situation has to be worked out one way or another because neither of us are leaving.

He meets me at the hallway with the same casual smile, the same 'nothing bothers me' attitude. He has the look of a guy who's always gotten everything he wanted in life and that's what attracted me to him in the first place.

He was one of the most serious relationships I've ever had and I actually saw myself marrying him.

On the way over to computer tech's office, I bury my head in my phone and avoid Thomas as much as I can while walking right next to him.

He keeps trying to start a conversation, but I brush him off, texting and composing an email.

We enter a long underground hallway that's a shortcut to the other building and he pulls on my hand and gets me to stop.

"Can we talk?" His eyes flicker in the dark and shadows cast along his face.

"No," I say. "I have nothing to say to you."

"We never really discussed what happened with Marissa."

I don't even want to hear her name, I say silently to myself.

"There's nothing to say. I don't want to be with a cheater and I think I made that perfectly clear."

"You did and I know that," he mumbles, "but I want you back."

I laugh.

It sounds more like a cough stuck in the back of my throat.

I start to turn around to walk away, but he grabs my hand again, pulling me close, and presses his lips to mine.

I shove him and he slams into the wall.

24

"**D**on't you ever touch me again," I say, trying to make my body as big as possible.

"I'm sorry." He runs up to me. "I'm sorry. I didn't mean to do that."

"Yes, you did. That's why you did it. You think it was romantic? Think you can just kiss me and everything will be fine?"

"No, I just thought the moment felt right."

"You don't know how to read moments," I say.

He nods.

That part is true, he doesn't.

"You got someone else pregnant when you were with me," I say, crossing my arms.

If he wants to talk about this, let's talk about it.

He takes a step back.

"You cheated on me and you asked her to marry you. Then you told me that you didn't want to be with me anymore. I got over that. I'm over you. I'm not going to waste any more time having this conversation."

"I know, but what if I told you I made a mistake? What if I told you that I don't want to be with her anymore? Marissa doesn't make me happy the way that you did."

"I would tell you that you have no idea what you're talking about. I would tell you that it doesn't make sense."

"It does, of course it does. I want you. I want you back. I want to go back to how everything was."

"You can't. There are consequences for your actions."

"Please forgive me," Thomas begs. His face falls and he reaches for me again.

"No."

I start to walk away, but he grabs my hand again. I brush him off.

"I miss you."

"What about that night?" I ask, anger rising within me.

His eyes narrow. He knows what I'm talking about.

"I should have called the cops on you," I hiss.

He swallows hard and admits, "I didn't mean for *that* to happen."

"You don't mean for anything to happen, but stuff keeps happening anyway whenever you're around. I refuse to be part of that anymore."

We stare at each other. I wait for him to say something else, to at least apologize for punching me in the stomach.

We were arguing just like this, then his eyes just flickered, something changed, and nothing was the same.

"Maybe you should have pressed charges," he says.

"You know how many people in this department would've taken your side? You know how far I'd be able to rise above this rank after that?"

He shrugs, but says nothing.

"I don't know why, but for some reason being hit as a woman is still considered to be your fault. Or perhaps maybe we should just get hit and not complain about it. I just hope that you didn't do that to Marissa."

"No, I didn't," he says. "She had a miscarriage at fifteen weeks."

"I'm sorry."

He shrugs and says, "Things were going off in the wrong direction even before then."

I'm tired of this.

I don't want to talk.

I don't want to relive all of the mistakes that I've made. I'm just glad that our time together has come to an end and that I didn't waste years on that loser and God forbid have any children with him.

He follows behind me all the way to the computer tech's office, who has a small place in the corner of the building across the way. Benjamin's out, but Samson's there.

I walk briskly ahead of Thomas, pushing him away with every step.

Samson is a small, diminutive guy who likes to make a lot of jokes that not many people understand.

I texted him earlier and he has everything open and ready on his laptop as soon as we arrive.

"Congratulations on your engagement," I say, giving Samson a hug.

"Oh, thank you. Expect an invitation. Both of you," he adds Thomas as a second thought.

I don't think that he would be invited if I hadn't brought it up and now I sort of wished that I hadn't.

"It's going to have an elfin theme, so wear a long dress and little elf ears if you can," Samson spices and Thomas doesn't even hide his cringe.

"Yes, of course." I nod, having no idea where I would get that kind of costume.

"I'll send you some websites with some good cosplay outfits," Sampson adds, reading my mind.

I always found it a little bit ironic that talking about the *Lord of the Rings* and *Star Wars* made you a geek but if you know all sorts of statistics about football, then you're just one of the cool guys.

Underneath his dress shirt, Samson has tattoos covering both arms. He wears thick glasses and has his long hair pulled up into a ponytail.

He's a little bit heavyset, but he recently started a workout regimen that he's posting about religiously on his social media.

What I like most about him is how confident he is in himself. I don't mean that as an insult. I love that he embraces everything that's a little bit weird about him. He's not embarrassed about anything.

Whenever I stand apart from others, I like to keep secrets. I don't want to share, like for instance, the fact that I like to read steam punk historical fiction books. It's silly, I guess, but what's wrong with having interests and what's wrong with being into things that are *unusual?*

"So, were you able to find anything interesting on Nick's or Janine's computers?" I ask after a little bit of small talk.

"They were friends, but from what I can tell from their texts and emails, which they shared a lot of those, they weren't romantic in the least."

"Not at all?"

"Nope. There's actually one email where Nick told her that he really appreciates her friendship and that he was sorry that he pulled away when she kissed him, but he's pursuing a celibate lifestyle to try and get his head more straight."

Then he shows us Janine's social media. Some pictures are pretty standard, but others are quite provocative if not bordering on explicit.

There are even a few in which she's almost completely nude, except has her arms placed in just the right locations to cover herself up.

"Wow, so Nick didn't have an interest in hooking up with her. Why not?" Thomas asks, suddenly revoking back to his fraternity brother ways.

"They seem to be very close friends," Samson says, being as professional as possible.

Samson opens the email that he was referring to and I read the word '*celibate*' and '*alone*' followed by *I promised myself that I'm not going to sleep with anyone for a year. Maybe then I'll actually be in a good headspace.*

"Man, what is wrong with kids today?" Thomas says.

Samson and I both look at him.

"I've heard about this a lot. There's so many twenty-somethings who are just not having sex. Like, do they actually think their problems can be solved by avoiding sex?" Thomas scoffs.

Samson and I exchange looks.

"You know, not everybody thinks that all of their problems can be solved with intercourse," I say.

"That's not what I remember about you," he says in a barely audible whisper when Samson is distracted.

I want to punch him in the mouth, but that would get me suspended, if not fired, and the right thing to do would be to file a report with human resources, stating that he said something to make it a hostile work environment.

The problem is that I work with a bunch of cops who make a lot of inappropriate jokes and it can be quite unsafe for me to start making these kind of reports.

25

The following morning, I meet with Sydney at her OBGYN appointment. I arrive early and she meets me in the parking lot. I walk up the stairs with her and even though she doesn't look pregnant everything suddenly feels different.

I don't want to burden her with what happened with Thomas, but she keeps asking because she saw the two of us together yesterday.

At first, I go over the highlights and then I splurge on the details. She's the only one who knows the truth about our relationship and everything thing that happened.

She listens carefully and gives me a hug.

"I'm really sorry that he's such a creep," she says.

I want to say, *I'm sorry that Patrick cheated on you, too. Some men are total pricks.*

I want to point out the fact that I'm no longer with Thomas, but I don't want to make her feel bad.

It's her decision to be with whomever she wants.

I keep having to remind myself of this fact.

It's hard to be supportive when you feel like your friend is making a mistake, but I don't know what else to do.

When we get to the office, the receptionist has Sydney fill out a lot of paperwork and then tells her that the doctor's running late so we can step out to get some coffee if we want.

"It will be at least twenty, maybe thirty more minutes," she informs us.

She takes Sydney's number and we head downstairs to the Starbucks. She orders a latte and I get a Darjeeling hot tea.

We sit on one of the comfy plush velvet chairs and we talk about everything and anything.

We catch up like we haven't in a while and it feels really good to talk to a friend. She asks me more about Thomas and how I feel.

"I just can't believe that he thought that he could just charm his way back in," I say. "He didn't even really apologize for putting his hands on me. He didn't even thank me for covering it up. I feel like such a fool."

"I'm so sorry." Sydney shakes her head.

"I wonder if he did that to Marissa. I wonder when he will do it to some future girlfriend and how she will feel, knowing that he did it to me. I just wish someone had warned me about him. Then I would have written him off a long time ago. What a waste of all my time."

Sydney nods, swirling the sugar using the wooden stick.

"I'm really happy for you. I mean, I know this was a really tough situation, but you handled it well. I know that you are kind of in a weird head space and I'm glad that you didn't get back together with him. He's not a good guy," she says, making the understatement of the century.

"I sometimes think back to how happy we were. I really thought that he got me. We laughed. We had the same sense of humor. I mean, he liked football a lot and a lot of other sports, but in general it felt like we were connected."

"Then he ended up being a cheater and worse."

"I just wish that I could know the truth. For a long time, I just dated people and didn't take anything seriously. That was fine but part of that is probably because of what happened to my dad." I mention him, but I don't go into any of the details now because Sydney already knows a lot.

"That's probably why you stayed away from long-term relationships. You didn't want to get hurt. You didn't want to be in the same situation that your mom was in."

"I just saw her compromising so much for love. She was always the one who was going the extra mile, forgiving him, taking him back, trying to make things right, and I was always angry with her. I always felt like she was covering for him in some way. I let it slip because, well, he was the only dad I had. So, when I grew up, I just thought that I don't want to be a woman like that, so maybe I'll just be a different type of woman, someone who didn't need a man."

"You don't."

"No, but it's nice having someone to talk to. It's nice to be with someone. Plus, I'm getting to a point in my life where I feel like I can't form an actual relationship with someone because of all these issues." I take a sip of my tea. "I really don't want to talk about all of this and I'm really sorry for ruining your appointment with all of this drama."

"No, not at all. First of all, I like drama," she says, "especially when it's not mine."

I smile out of the corner of my lips.

"To be serious, it's a nice reprieve. I like having something else to think about besides my own problems."

My phone rings and I look down on the screen to see that it's Luke. I don't want to take it, but Sydney leans over and insists.

"What if there's a development in the case? You have to take it. I'll be right here."

I nod and answer reluctantly.

It's not that I don't want to talk to him and it's not that I don't want to hear about developments, it's just that I'm afraid.

I'm afraid that he will say that they found her and that she's no longer alive. It seems like for as long as she's missing, there's still hope, but once there's a body, that's it. There can only be justice or maybe vengeance, but that's it.

Luke's voice is monotone and professional.

He quickly gets to the point because he knows me well enough and he has been doing his job long enough to know that people in my position tend to hold their breath, waiting for an update.

"There isn't anything new," he says almost immediately. "No developments, no additional leads."

"What does that mean?" I ask, my mouth becoming like cotton.

"You know what it means," he says quietly,

I swallow hard but because my mouth is so dry, I cough. The case is going cold.

This was the first time that I have ever allowed myself to think this way. When a case goes cold, it means resources dry up. It means attention gets diverted to other cases and hope starts to dwindle.

It doesn't mean that anything is impossible and that you can't find out what happened, but it's not so much of an active investigation and other things take priority.

Obviously, it's not as bad as finding a body, but then again, after enough time, you kind of assume that there should be a body and you almost want to find one to put everything to bed.

"How are you?" Luke asks, turning on FaceTime.

He leans the camera close to his face and I can see the twinkle in his eyes.

I pull mine away, aware of the oppressive fluorescent light that makes me look washed out and like I have big dark circles under my eyes.

"I have to come up there and canvas. I have to ask more people more questions."

"The deputy has done that."

"I know, but you know how it is, sometimes when the victim's family member does it or sometimes right after the crime happens, people don't want to come forward. Later on, they have some doubts."

"They do. You can do that," Luke says, "but it's going to be very tedious work."

"Are you saying that I shouldn't do it because it's boring?" I snap at him.

I don't mean it, but I'm suddenly taking everything he says personally.

"No, not at all. I think it's a good idea. I'm just saying that I get the sense from the department, from my boss that they don't know what's going to happen. Do you know what that means?"

"What?" I whisper.

Our eyes meet.

He clenches his jaw and relaxes. He licks his lips and slowly opens his mouth.

"It means that the first opportunity there's another case somewhere else that's more pressing, that's more able to be solved, they're going to send me there."

I nod.

I understand that this is how his job works.

Frankly, this is how *my* job works.

If we don't find out what happened to Nick Millian soon, there's going to be another murder, more people to interrogate, and my attention will be diverted to that.

I'll still interview and we'll still conduct the DNA analysis and whatever evidence can be gathered from the body, but if the murder isn't solved relatively quickly, it's put aside and other cases, more solvable ones, take precedence.

Television shows, books, and movies will have you believe that detectives work on all cases until they're solved. The truth is that there are currently about 250,000 unsolved murders in the United States and the number increases by about 6,000 each year.

The Department of Justice calls this a crisis of cold cases. The FBI estimates that investigators are only able to close about 62% of murder cases and 35% of sexual assaults in 2017.

The number of unsolved violent crimes, which eventually become known as cold cases, increases year after year.

I have a number of them in files on the computer on my desk, but new files come along so new people have to be interviewed and new crimes have to be solved. The thing is that you have to do it very quickly because witnesses disappear or forget and evidence, if there is any, is never processed and often lost.

That's right, I said what I said. DNA evidence isn't as common as you think. It's not a magic bullet and there are a lot more cases like my sister's where there's simply no forensic evidence at all.

I tell Luke that I'm going to be back to Big Bear soon and I'll let him know when.

"I'd like to have dinner or lunch, if you're available," I add.

"Yeah, I'd like that, too," he says with a smile. "I've missed you."

I nod. I should tell him that I missed him, too, because it's the truth, but the words are hard for me to get out.

"Okay. I'll be in touch." I nod and hang up.

When I get back to the Starbucks, I see Sydney sitting on Patrick's lap, dressed in a suit jacket and a button-down shirt.

He holds his hand on her stomach, like a proud expectant dad.

I'm shocked to see him, but I put on my best poker face, plastering a smile on my face, and giving him a warm hug.

"Congratulations," I say. "Thanks for coming out here."

Patrick runs his fingers through his hair, a nervous habit of his, either that or he just wants to bring attention to just how gorgeous it is.

"I actually have somewhere to go, so now that you're here, I'll be on my way."

"No, don't go." Sydney grabs my hand, but I pull away.

"The two of you should share this time together," I whisper, giving her a squeeze of the hand and kissing her on the cheek.

When I watch her shoulder disappear in his embrace, I'm genuinely happy for them and I hope that it all works out.

26

The following morning, I oversleep.

I feel myself getting sick. I'm congested, my throat hurts, and my lips feel dry. I drink some water and wash my face, but I can't move as quickly as I want to.

Everything is somewhat in slow motion and my head spins when I try to speed up. I'm tempted to call in sick, but I have an interview to get to that can't be rescheduled.

I don't have time for a shower, so I throw on some dry shampoo, brush it out to get rid of the white spots, and put on a little bit of makeup to try to hide my dark circles under my eyes.

Three Advil isn't enough to take the headache and make it go away, but it takes the edge off a little bit.

When I get to the precinct, I realize that Thomas has already started the interview without me.

I'm annoyed. This isn't procedure.

I stop by the video conferencing room where deputies and Captain Medvil are watching everything unfold on an enormous screen. The captain doesn't explicitly mention my tardiness, but the sour expression on his face conveys that fact nevertheless.

Then he points to the screen and I watch for a few minutes while Thomas questions Danny, this time in a much more harsh and less hospitable way.

"You see what happens when you don't show up on time," Captain Medvil says, his voice tinged with disappointment.

"I'm sorry. I'm getting sick and I didn't get much sleep."

"Not my problem." Medvil swivels his chair toward the screen and points to Thomas leaning over Danny. "Did you two discuss him playing bad cop this whole time?"

"No, not at all."

He's been practically yelling at him and from the looks on Danny's face, he's not going to put up with it much longer.

"Let me go in and talk to him."

Medvil hesitates for a second. I don't know why, the plan was for us to talk to him at the same time, so what's different?

"Put the earpiece in," he says. "Thomas doesn't have one, so we can't calm him down."

Now, it's my turn to hesitate.

"Do it and you better get in there fast. That kid looks like he's going to crack and ask for a lawyer."

A deputy hands me a small waxy piece to go into my ear. It's on Bluetooth and I drop my hair down to cover it. They've only been a mainstay in the department for the last few years and I can't say that I'm completely comfortable with wearing one.

It's one thing to listen to music or a podcast when you're going on with your life like doing grocery shopping or having some coffee, but it's a whole other thing to have the captain bark orders at you while you're trying to talk to someone in an authoritative way and not have them notice that you're actually taking orders from someone else.

"You have to quit lying to me!" Thomas yells at Danny.

"I'm not. I already told you everything. I don't know anything about Nick or Janine."

"That's not true. You know it. I know it. Eve knows it."

"Eve doesn't know anything!" Danny yells.

Danny stands up and starts to gather his things. It's almost too late. I rush around to the door to that room where they're in when I hear a loud thrust. Thomas has put his hand through the drywall.

I open the door just as he pulls it out with an expression of shock and awe on his face. His eyes look like they're practically bugging out of his skull. His skin is white, devoid of all blood, and yet there's still anger there, more than before.

Thomas looks down at his bleeding hand and he practically crumbles to the floor. Suddenly, I'm taken back to that moment when he did that to me, only there was no drywall.

He punched me really hard just like that. The anger started rising and rising within him and then he couldn't make it stop.

I can say that it was someone else doing it. I can say that some sort of darkness took him over, but I don't know if that would be true.

This is Thomas.

This is a part of him.

When he did that to me, we were just having an argument. I didn't call him any names and I can't even remember what we were talking about. Then suddenly, he just kept getting more and more pissed off when I refused to agree. That's when the violence exploded out of him.

I turn toward Danny and I'm at a loss for words. I look back at Thomas who walks out of the door and slams it behind him.

He's off the case and he will be lucky if Danny doesn't press charges or ask for an attorney right here and right now.

I lick my lips and grab onto the Manila folder in front of me, tighter to try to calm down my breathing.

Where do I take this now?

Do I keep going or do I stop?

I'm afraid that if I let him go now, he'll have some time to think about this and he'll get angry at Thomas.

Maybe he'll come back here with an attorney and take his badge. Perhaps he deserves that. No, I know that he does, but he's also a good cop.

"What are you doing just standing there?" Captain Medvil shouts into my ear, shutting down my stream of consciousness. "Talk to him, comfort him, and show him that you're nothing like Thomas."

"I'm really sorry about that," I say in a quiet, reserved way.

"Is that who you have to work with all the time?"

"Luckily not all the time," I say, "but yeah, he works in the department."

"God, I'm sorry. He's a nutcase. I mean, he punched the wall."

I look him up and down. Combat boots, black t-shirt. A head that's been shaved since the last time I saw him with an attractive undercut.

Tattoos up and down his arms and a metal dog collar around his neck. If he's trying to look scary to an everyday person, then he is succeeding and yet, he's the one that looks terrified of Thomas.

The irony is not lost on me.

"I think I want to see an attorney," Danny says after I ask him to sit down.

"Make him reconsider," Captain Medvil whispers into my ear.

"Can I just talk to you about a few things? I'm really sorry about what he just did, but I just wanted to clear up a few things and then this'll be over."

That seems to put him at ease.

Still eyeing the hole in the wall, he agrees to sit down. I put him on the other side of the table so that he's facing the other camera and doesn't have to constantly look at the indentation in the drywall.

I ask him about knowing Janine.

"You told me before that you've never met her, but your girlfriend..."

"Fiancée," he corrects me.

"Your fiancée. She told me otherwise."

"Yeah, I think she's right," Danny says with a shrug.

He leans back in his chair, sticking his leg out to relax. It's almost as if what happened only a few moments before was something that he watched in a movie.

His ability to transition between emotional states makes me a little bit uncomfortable.

"Can I ask you what your interactions with Janine have been now that you remember more?"

"Yeah, I think we met a few times at either a party that he had or I had."

"What kind of parties were these?"

"Uh, nothing really formal, just some beers, karaoke, and sometimes a game."

"What was your impression of Janine?"

"I just kind of saw her in the kitchen. I think she was fixing the keg one time. Then another time I saw her dancing. She was a pretty girl, but we never really had much of an interaction."

"Okay, got it," I say.

Looking through my notes, I feel a little bit uncomfortable sitting here in front of him with my back completely straight, dressed in a suit jacket, matching black pants, and heels.

My head starts to feel cloudy again and I can't help but sneeze. I search my bag for a tissue and luckily, find one to blow my nose.

"Sorry about that," I say, leaning away from him.

I feel flushed and hot, but I can't take off my jacket because the shirt underneath is drenched with sweat. Instead, I take a sip from my bottle of water and try to gather my thoughts.

"You know, Nick was always such a great guy," Danny says. "We had such a good time and it's just too bad that he's not around."

I nod.

"I just wonder why he would do this to her. I didn't get the sense that they were together. Maybe they were just friends, but why kill her?"

"Yeah, I don't know either. That's what we're trying to find out. Was he angry at her possibly?"

27

Danny sighs, narrowing his eyes. He runs his hands through his hair and then looks right at me again.

"Um, I don't know. He could have been. One thing I was thinking about is what if he attacked her? What if he tried to sleep with her or something and she wasn't into it and he raped her anyway?"

"Could he have done that?" I ask.

"I wouldn't think so, but you never know. He seemed to be such a nice guy, but you never know with people."

"So, your theory is what exactly?"

"Well, he's gone and you found her dead in his apartment. He probably killed her. As to why, I don't know. Just wondering if maybe he raped her and then things got a little bit out of control. Maybe she threatened to call the police and he got scared so he just shot her and then shot himself."

My mouth drops open.

"Shot himself?! Shot himself?!" Medvil yells in my ear. "He never said this before. Call him on it now!"

I hate having this earpiece in. He's drowning out my thoughts with his voice, but in this case, Medvil's voice is like the sound of my own conscience.

"Keep him talking," he continues. "Why? Why does he think that Nick is dead?"

"Um, why do you think that he's dead?" I ask, trying to be as casual and nonchalant about what he has just mentioned as possible.

I don't want to draw attention to having him worry about revealing something unusual, but the other thing that I noticed is that he has already talked about Nick in past tense.

That's usually not something people do unless they have certain knowledge that someone is no longer with us.

"I was just thinking out loud. I don't know. I mean, maybe he just ran away and is hiding out somewhere."

"He hasn't touched any of his money or any of his bank accounts though."

"Well, he probably knows that you can trace that and his phone, so maybe he's hiding out for real."

"He did have a lot of money in his bank account," I say. "Did you know that?"

"Yeah, he actually mentioned that to me."

"He did?" I ask, surprised.

"Yeah, he had a lot of money saved up from being overseas."

"I still don't quite understand how Kenny Tuffin is involved in this. You paid him in pizza to use Nick's card to get money out of his account, but why, if he promised to give you the money?"

"Well, I knew that you'd be tracking his bank stuff and credit cards. I needed to get that money back, so I didn't want it to be traced to me, but I guess you found it anyway."

"Yeah, we did and now you mentioned that Nick might be dead, so of course that sparks my interest."

Our eyes meet again and I wait for him to look away first.

"Yeah, I know. I was just talking, you know?" Danny says casually, completely unfazed. "I was just so shocked to see that he had murdered Janine that I wasn't sure what was going to happen."

"So, what makes you think that Nick is dead now?"

"I don't think that exactly, but it seems like an obvious turn of events, right?"

"How so?" I ask.

I run my fingers along the outside of the folder and feel the smooth pressure of it on my tips. Another sneeze comes on, but I fight it to keep the tension in the moment.

My eyes begin to water and I press the tissue to my nose, trying to keep everything at bay.

"I think he's afraid. I think he *was* afraid," Danny says, twirling his thumbs. He intertwines his fingers and continues the circular motion, almost as though it were a nervous tic.

"Afraid of what?" I ask.

I can hear the clicking of his heel on the linoleum floor.

Thump.

Thump.

Thump.

He's speeding up slightly with each collision.

"I don't think you'd be surprised if I told you that I think that Nick killed Janine," Danny finally says, bringing his eyes to mine. "He killed her and ran away and maybe killed himself. Of course, it's just my opinion."

———

AFTER DANNY UTTERS THOSE WORDS, I look at him for a while. His irises shift just a little, but whatever nervousness he exhibited earlier vanishes and I wonder if it were all an act.

Everything that he told me is hypothetical, but this is how it starts. At first, I get him to reveal a possibility of what could have happened and then we start to etch out the truth.

"Good job," Captain Medvil whispers into my ear. "Keep him talking. Get him to say more."

"Do you have any idea where Nick could have gone?" I ask. "I mean, you two were close."

"No, I wouldn't say that. We were neighbors and kind of friendly, but I didn't know much about his personal life. I didn't even know about Janine."

"Well, you knew that they were friendly."

"Yeah, but I had no idea that he could do something like that."

He leans back in his chair again, the arrogance pulling toward the surface.

"Well, you seem to be one of his closest friends because we couldn't find anyone online or in person that he spent more time with. So, would you have any idea where he could have gone?"

"He did mention Montana, but then again, he also mentioned Mexico."

I nod. He's trying to throw me off course here.

What I still don't know, however, is exactly how many details he's aware of.

Is he covering for his friend?

Is Nick sending him money to protect him for what he did?

Is there something else going on?

"Listen, Danny, I know that you're trying to be helpful, but is there anything else? Is there somewhere he liked to hang out at like a special place that he would go?"

"Well, if you are assuming that he's alive."

"You're not?" I ask.

He hadn't mentioned Nick possibly being dead now a number of times enough to not let me ignore it.

"Yeah. I was worried about that. Nick would have these dark moods. He would get really depressed. You told me how Eve told you about what he said to her. He lost his friend and he felt like he should have been the one who was killed out there in that Humvee. He had kind of a death wish."

"What does that mean?" I ask. "Was he driving too fast? Being reckless? What?"

"I think he just snapped." Danny shrugs. "That's probably why Janine got killed. Maybe regret and remorse set in so he couldn't deal with that anymore. He's a very sweet guy. He thinks a lot about people and animals. He has a lot of empathy. So knowing that he did that to his friend, that would be really difficult for him."

"I feel like you're trying to tell me something, Danny," I say. "You know that you're not going to be in trouble. If you know where Nick is, I can protect you."

Danny casts his eyes onto the Formica table and picks at a crack in the corner. His nails are painted black and chipping off in big flakes, yet he digs into the crevice before looking up at me.

"Nick is my friend and I promised him that I would protect him."

"I know, but you also owe something to Janine's family. They need closure. They need to know what happened to their daughter and sister."

"Good job. Keep him talking," Medvil whispers in my ear like I don't know that.

I want him to shut up and stop from distracting me but Danny doesn't know about the earpiece and I need to keep it that way.

28

I want to keep talking to Danny, but it's also not lost on me the fact that he had already asked for a lawyer.

He had asked for an attorney and I had essentially talked him out of it. It was kind of a casual asking and I don't know exactly if it will stand up in court. But if it does go there and we get an ornery judge, then that part of his testimony can be thrown out along with any other findings that it leads to.

Medvil wants me to keep talking because he forgets about stuff like that. I know that he's the captain, but a lot of his cases have come close to being thrown out on technicalities. That angers him, but that's also what makes him kind of a sloppy detective.

I need to do better.

"You know the other detective? He really freaked me out," Danny says. "I can't believe that he punched the wall like that."

"Yeah, I'm really sorry about that. That was so unprofessional."

"Unprofessional would be an understatement. How about violent? Scary? Maybe even a fireable offense, huh?"

I shrug my shoulders.

"You're telling me that he can't get fired over doing something like that?"

"It would definitely go on his record," I say, "but it's not really up to me."

"You will testify if I make a complaint, right?"

"Let's not talk about that right now. Let's talk about Nick," I say, trying to gear the conversation back to what I need.

The last thing that I can think about right now is whether or not anything is going to happen to Thomas at a disciplinary hearing.

"You know, Thomas told me that I didn't need an attorney. Is that true?"

"No, I wouldn't say that."

"Shut up!" Medvil yells.

I swallow hard trying to ignore him.

"I mean, that you're right, but it would make things a little more complicated for you. Look, Danny, from how it looks here, you haven't done anything wrong. You're just helping me find your friend who may be responsible for what happened to Janine or maybe not. He may be hiding out for nothing. He might've come home, found her there, freaked out, and disappeared thinking that people would think that he did it, but forensic evidence and circumstantial evidence might point to a stranger altogether. I have no idea. That's why I'm trying to gather all of this information. That's why I'm trying to get to the bottom of this."

Ninety percent of what I said is just a story. It's a casual kind of thing that a cop tells someone that they interview in order to put them at peace and to keep them talking, but I do realize that I'm making a mistake.

If Danny says something to me now after I told him that he doesn't need an attorney, his lawyer is going to have a very strong case to get that testimony thrown out.

"Would you like something to eat?" I ask. "My stomach is growling."

"Yeah. I could have some pretzels and M&M's." Danny smiles. "Also some Sprite if you have an extra seventy-five cents."

"My treat," I say. "I'll be right back."

I head over straight to the video conferencing room where I'm relieved to see the assistant district attorney, Katherine Harris.

She looks tired and overworked from having way too many cases in a day, but she's here and I appreciate it.

"You shouldn't have said that," Katherine says, shaking her head. "You shouldn't have told him that he didn't need a lawyer after the second time that he asked."

"I know."

"You also do not want to deny them their rights. Anyway, so far, I think you're in the clear. Just get him to say that he doesn't want a lawyer. Get him to affirmatively say those two words, 'No lawyer,' and then keep him talking."

I don't have much time.

I head over to the vending machine, get what he ordered, and grab myself a pack of pretzels and a coffee as well. I wish to God that I could take off this jacket, but when I reach over, I can see that my pit stains are practically down to my waist.

My shirt is drenched. I can't let him see me sweat, quite literally. This didn't just happen from talking to him. I often get sweaty when I'm in a cold room and when I have to interact with strangers.

I have a low grade of anxiety that used to be a lot higher grade and unmanageable, but now has settled into this point. I can relax enough to make it bearable, but I'm never fully relaxed.

I hand Danny his food and we dig in, eating in silence for a few moments. He's ravenous and drinks the Sprite in three big gulps. I know that I need to get him to say that he doesn't want a lawyer, but I don't know exactly how to do that without arousing suspicion.

"Listen, since you asked for a lawyer, I can't really keep this conversation going."

"Oh, okay." He looks a little disappointed.

"Unless you want to. I mean, there's still a few things that I think you can help me with, but I first need something from you."

"What? What is it?" he asks, chewing with his mouth open, crunching loudly and tossing handfuls of M&M's into his mouth.

"Well, you kind of have to say that you don't want the lawyer anymore out loud. Otherwise, this interview has to come to an end."

"What the…" Captain Medvil yells in my ear, but I reach over and turn him off.

I return my gaze to Danny and wait calmly for his answer.

"Okay. Yeah. That's fine." He nods, shrugging it off.

"No, you actually have to say it," I say, taking a gulp of my coffee.

Is this actually going to work?

"Oh. Okay. No, I want to keep talking to you without an attorney." He nods and I want to reach over to give him a big hug, but I don't.

Instead, I give him a casual smile.

"So, I was thinking about something," I say carefully, choosing my words. "I was thinking maybe you're covering up for Nick. Like, you know where he is and you don't want to tell anyone, which would make you an accessory to murder if he did indeed kill that girl. The other thing that I was thinking..." He raises his eyebrows to look at me. "...is that maybe he attacked you."

"Attacked me?"

"Yeah. Maybe you saw something that you weren't supposed to. Maybe you were defending yourself?"

"No. I wasn't there. I have no idea what you're talking about."

"Are you sure?" I ask. "The crime scene report came back and they found your footprints in his living room."

"What?"

I nod.

"No. I was his friend. So obviously, I was there at one point."

"They're searching your apartment now, but there were two footprints that match your size and style of shoe in the blood just in the hallway leading from the living room. I believe that they're yours."

This is what I've been waiting for.

This is what I've been setting up this whole conversation about. The suspect is caught off guard. He doesn't have time to think.

He doesn't suspect a thing. He thinks someone is on his side the whole time and that's when I can gauge his true reaction.

I can see if he is really surprised that I would think something like that because he didn't do it.

Is he shocked to hear me mention that because in reality, he is involved?

Danny's face becomes white.

Blood starts to drain away from it. He interlaces his fingers again. He starts to nervously stomp his heel on the floor.

It's very quiet at first, barely noticeable, but I know now that it's a tic of his. It's something he does to pass the time the same way he runs his middle finger on top of the nail of his pointer finger over and over again to try to calm himself down.

"Listen, I don't want to put words in your mouth," I say, "but I want to hear the truth from you. I know that you're helping your friend, but I also know that your friend has military experience and a history of violence. The government trained him to be violent and a lot of those people come back from a war and the world becomes kind of a gray place for them. There isn't the same black and white world of right and wrong that we live in."

"Yeah. I was there," Danny says, nods, and swallows hard.

I see his Adam's apple travel up and down the length of his throat.

"It was like what you said. I walked in and I sort of surprised him. I thought we would just hang out. His door was open and that's when I saw her lying there in his bedroom. You couldn't see her from the living room, so I had no way of knowing that anything happened."

"What about the sound from the gunshot?"

"I don't know. There's always ambulances and helicopters outside and people playing their music too loud. I just thought it was maybe a car backfiring."

"So, you came in and what happened?"

"I walked into the living room and I called his name. I saw that the lights were on everywhere, so he must've been home. I took a few steps into the hallway and that's when I saw her foot. I just... I should've just turned around and walked out, but I didn't."

"What did you do?" I ask.

"Nick freaked out. He... No, I can't talk about this," Danny says.

"Danny, please."

"I can't. I... This is... I need to talk to Eve. I... I have to talk to an attorney. No, I can't talk to you about this. I said too much."

With that, he gets up and walks out. There's nothing I can do.

I try to catch up with him in the hallway, but it's too late. He knows that I can't arrest him.

What would I even arrest him on?

I don't even know what the story is, but he apologized again and again. Then he says that he can't say anything else.

After he walks out the front door, I head toward Captain Medvil, DA Katherine Harris, and all of the deputies spill out of the video conferencing room.

They stare at me and I stare at them and they begin to clap.

"Good job!" Katherine says with a smile. "You got him to take back asking for a lawyer and then admit all of that. Great freaking job!"

"What do we do now?" I ask.

"We're going to try to find something," Captain Medvil says. "By the way, that thing about his footprints, that was pure gold, but that was hell of a chance that you took."

"Why? What're you talking about?" Katherine asks.

"We don't have any footprints," I explain. "I mean, none of the stuff from the lab came back yet. I just got this feeling that maybe he was there or he knew something more about it, so I wanted to tell him about some evidence that we had and see what he would say."

"That's a dangerous game you played." Katherine smiles approvingly.

I inhale and exhale slowly, trying to get my head to stop from spinning. The Advil wore off many hours ago and I know that I'm due for a new dose.

My nose starts to run and I sneeze and everyone in the room takes a few steps away from me.

"I'm really sorry," I say, realizing just how congested I sound and look. "I don't want to get all of you sick."

"Yeah. So, in that case, you better go home," Captain Medvil instructs. "You did good. Let's try to figure this out and get some more evidence. Hopefully we'll get somewhere. Maybe we'll bring his fiancée in for a little chat, but only after he talks to her a little bit more."

"Sounds like a good plan." I start to cough.

My throat closes up and I know that it's time for me to go.

29

I meet up with Thomas again in the break room, not because I want to, but because he's there and certain things have to be talked about. When I look at him through the glass, he looks broken and lost.

I'm sure that he's having lots of regrets for putting his fist through the wall with a suspect, especially one that wasn't being violent or aggressive at all, but this is how Thomas is.

Few people at work know he's had a few disciplinary actions. People who he has arrested have come up and said that he was unnecessary violent with them, but you know how it is when you have a little bit of crack, marijuana, or heroin in your pocket. Suddenly your testimony becomes a lot less reliable.

I walk in and clear my throat. He's facing away, sitting with his back to me. Once he sees that it's me, his eyes flare up.

"I'm assuming you finished the conversation," he says.

"Yes, of course. What else was I going to do?"

He shrugs.

"Why did you do that?" I ask. "Why did you attack him like that?"

"I didn't attack him. I attacked the wall. Listen, if I wanted to punch him in the face, I would have."

I shake my head.

I can't believe that someone like this is still on the force.

He's not particularly good at interrogating. He's not particularly good at investigating.

He just has friends in the right places and he has been here long enough to keep working.

I wouldn't be surprised if in the future, he ends up killing someone who's unarmed for no reason whatsoever.

I can't make any of these thoughts public.

I can't talk to anyone about this, not even Internal Affairs, because that would put a bullseye on my back. Cops watch out for their own and, in this job, you need others to protect you in dangerous situations.

The one thing that Thomas has is a lot of friends. A lot more than I do. It's not that I'm not friendly. It's that female detectives are still not completely trusted by everyone.

Thomas is gregarious, fun, and he knows how to have a good time and cover everyone's tab at the strip club, the kind of place that the female officers aren't exactly invited to.

I don't know if this is what it's like everywhere, but this is what it's like here.

"Listen, you don't need to be here and gloat over what happened, okay?"

"I'm not gloating. I'm here to see if you're okay, because clearly you kind of lost it for a moment."

"I didn't lose anything!" He yells back.

"You didn't? So, you meant to put your fist through the wall?"

"Shut up," he growls. "You stupid bitch."

I know that this conversation isn't going to go anywhere productive. He's not in the mood.

"Well, that could have gone better." Katherine comes in with a casual smile on her face.

She looks almost amused by the situation. She has always seemed to have a sixth sense when it comes to Thomas Abrams because she has never been a big fan.

When we dated, I noticed that she stayed away from me. I wonder how much she knew. She remained friendly, cordial, and professional as always, but not particularly going out of her way to include me in any trips to the bar.

"Listen, I know I messed up," Thomas says, turning around and throwing his hands up.

He's sitting at the white Formica table. He has a can of Coke in front of him. He finishes it with a few big gulps and throws it in the trash. He misses, but then doesn't pick it up.

Katherine and I exchange glances and wait.

Finally, embarrassed for doing something wrong, he forces himself up to his feet and throws it away as if he had meant to do it all along.

That's how it has always been with him. You practically have to shame him to do anything that's right, polite, or according to rules of society.

"You know, we're going to be lucky if Danny doesn't press charges," Katherine says.

She leans against the counter and her pencil skirt scrunches up just a little bit, but it's tailored so nicely that it still looks very form-fitting and exquisite.

Assistant district attorneys don't make a lot of money and usually can't afford nice clothing like this in addition to rent and everything else that goes in to living in a big city.

She's still paying off her student loans, but she cares about fashion and presenting herself well. Her hair is always styled and her makeup is always flawless.

"Listen, isn't there anything that we can do?" Thomas asks. "I mean, maybe the camera stopped working at that moment and there's no record of what happened."

"Even if that had happened, we have all seen what you did," Katherine says, crossing her arms in front of her. "What are you asking us to do exactly, Officer Abrams?"

He starts to huff and his face starts to resemble that of a petulant child.

It's like he has been told that the world works one way and is suddenly surprised, but it doesn't.

Maybe he would've never even become a cop if he knew that things were at least moving in the right direction in terms of not being such a corrupt and toxic workplace environment.

A few moments later, Captain Medvil joins us.

"What the hell was that?" he asks, spreading his feet out in a wider stance and placing his hands on his hips in that commonplace cop stance.

"Nothing. It was just a mistake," Thomas apologizes without really apologizing.

"Well, that's completely unacceptable," Captain Medvil barks back. "We don't do that kind of stuff here, you know that. We don't threaten or agitate suspects in a physical way. Do you know why?"

I know what Thomas is thinking. He wants to say because you're a pushover and this department has too many women in it.

Captain Medvil tilts his head and says, "It's not the right thing to do and because suspects like that, they get lawyers and then don't tell us a thing. Then they go and tell their friends that you can just act out, get punched, and then get off scot-free of all your charges because a police officer was violent with you. No, we don't do that anymore. You know that, I know that, hell, you're a young guy. We haven't done that kind of thing in a long time, so don't pretend that you don't know what kind of world you're living in."

Thomas shrugs and mumbles something, but it's not legible and it's hard to make out.

When the captain leaves, Katherine follows soon after and we're left alone again.

I don't want to stay here any longer than necessary so I head toward the door, but Thomas rushes up to me.

"You did that on purpose." He puts his finger in my face and cold sweat rushes down my back.

I have a flashback to what happened before, to him putting his hands on me, threatening me, to all the put downs that he said to me, to all the times that he made me think that I wasn't good enough.

"You're a stupid little bitch," Thomas whispers in my ear. "You made me do that on purpose, but you're not going to get away with it."

"What? What did I make you do on purpose?" I ask, taking a little step away from the wall, just in case he slams me into it. "I wasn't even there. You were there all alone and you let your anger and your frustration and all of your emotions out on that guy. When all you have to do to get him to talk is to connect with him, to make him feel safe, to make him feel like you're his friend, but you couldn't do that, could you?"

Now it's his turn to take a little step back. He knows I'm right.

I see his whole body deflate, just a little. I see him.

It's almost as if he's a balloon, just letting the air out of itself.

Being around Thomas is like being around a bomb that's about to explode. You make the wrong move or you say just the wrong thing at the wrong moment and it will explode in your face.

I said my peace, but now I slide carefully parallel to the wall to not agitate him and to not make it seem like an act of aggression.

There's no recording of our conversation here and who knows how he can spin it.

I need to play my cards right. This is a game of poker and it requires strategy. I walk around him, open the door, walk out, and I don't let out a breath until the door closes behind me.

"What's going on with you two?" Katherine walks up to me and I nearly jump out of my skin.

I exhale in a quick burst and she licks her lips slowly, assessing the situation.

"Nothing. Just... Some professional differences."

"Yeah, it's more than that," Katherine says, tilting her head to one side and crossing her arms across her chest.

I don't know her well and she has always been cordial. The fact that she doesn't like Thomas is a good thing, but I still don't know who to trust.

"Did something happen? Did he do something to you?"

I swallow hard and ask, "What are you talking about? No, of course not." My protest is hardly believable or honest.

She bites her lower lip again, and then calls me into her office.

"I need to talk to you," she says.

As I follow her across the room, past all the cubicles, it feels a lot like I've been called into the principal's office.

30

Katherine Harris's office is on the other side of the building. It has a beautiful view of the LA skyline. The door is made of dark wood to match the rest of the outside, but inside I find an office that's light and very easy when it comes to décor.

There are no heavy dark colors, there's no ornate furniture, and there's no grandiose artwork. There are three matching pictures on the wall looking out the window.

They are sepia in color and minimalist in style, each one portraying a different type of plant. A cactus, a eucalyptus, and a third one that I can't quite identify.

The focus is zoomed up close and personal, the background is blank, and the frames are all slim in a white ash wood.

Her diploma from Southwestern Law School hangs in a similar style frame on the other side of the wall. Her bachelor's degree from University of Southern California with a major in philosophy is right below that.

"I went there, too," I say.

"Oh, yes, that's right." She smiles. "I remember you told me that when we went out for drinks."

I nod.

We talked for maybe a few minutes. Going out with a group, I always find it hard to get a word in.

There are two wall bookcases, slim and nondescript, reminding me of the IKEA ones popular in the nineties. A sparse number of law books are stacked one on top of another, separated by more cacti and even a few novels.

The desk itself is uncluttered. Just a laptop, an iPad, a small wireless keyboard, and a notebook. On the right-hand side, there's a stack of folders in a plastic organizer.

She sits down on the swivel chair across from me, pointing to the small blue one in the front.

"Wow. This one is surprisingly comfortable," I say, spinning around in a half crescent.

"Yeah. I like it. It doesn't look like it would be so people don't tend to hang around for long."

I smile.

"Listen, I don't mean to call you out on anything. I just wanted to chat," she says. "I thought here we could be a little bit more comfortable."

I nod, not entirely sure what that means.

"Tell me about Thomas." She shifts her weight from one side to another.

Even though she's wearing a pretty tight jacket, she doesn't remove it.

"What do you want to know?"

"Well, to tell you the truth, you didn't seem very surprised by what he did."

"You mean punching the wall?"

She nods.

"I guess I'm kind of aware of his temper," I say.

"I just wish that someone told me about it," she points out.

"What do you mean?"

"Well, when I asked Captain Medvil about it, that's kind of what he said. I wouldn't have sent Thomas in there to talk to Danny at all if I knew that."

"I'm sorry. I didn't think it was my place," I say, feeling like I'm being scolded.

"Of course, it's your place."

"Things are very complicated with Thomas. I'm his colleague."

"Things like what? Our reputation is all we have. Especially in this department, people have to know who they're working with," Katherine says. "Maybe he's not a good candidate to interview and interrogate, but that doesn't mean that he's not a good cop. That doesn't mean that there isn't a place for him to do something else."

"He's a detective," I say, leaning back in my chair with a smirk on my face. "If he can't interview people, there isn't much of a place for him to do anything."

She smiles out of the corner of her lips. Her face is slim with high cheekbones and perfectly arched eyebrows.

There's a pleasantness to the expression on her face though. She isn't cold or distant. She's someone that you can relate to even though she is quite beautiful.

"I got the sense that you and Thomas were close?"

"I don't know how to answer that question," I say.

"Did you ever date?"

I want to lie. Maybe it would be my best professional interest to do so but something tells me to trust her.

"I'd rather not talk about that," I say. "Things were a little bit complicated and it's better to just leave it alone."

"Not if you have previous knowledge of him being violent and aggressive."

I freeze up. She knows something, but what?

How could she? I didn't tell anyone about it.

"Look, Kaitlyn, we haven't had much of a chance to spend time together. If I tell you this, then I need to swear you to secrecy. Can I trust you?"

"Yes, of course," I say, shaking my head.

She narrows her eyes like she doesn't believe me.

"If you were to tell anyone about this, then we would have a real professional problem on our hands. It would be your word against mine and I will deny it, I hope you know that."

"Deny what?"

"Do I have your word?" she asks again.

"Yes." I nod, staring straight into her wide brown eyes, feeling my hands getting clammy and cold.

"Well, the thing is that Thomas is not a very nice person and I have a feeling that you know that."

It's almost as if my blood starts rushing through my veins.

Everything stops.

The world even stops spinning. The only constant that remains is a strange buzzing sound somewhere in the distance and with every passing moment, it gets louder and louder.

"I'm not sure what to say," I mumble after a very long pause.

"Thomas and I have history," Katherine finally says. "We dated a long time ago and things didn't go well. This was before I even went to law school."

"Oh."

"I had just graduated. I took a year off. I was working doing legal defense kind of stuff, trying to figure out if I wanted to go to law school or not. I just took the LSAT exam. I was doing all the applications. We were dating and... Well, not really dating."

"What do you mean?" I ask.

"We were friends. We knew each other. I went out to a bar with him and his friends and someone slipped me something."

"How do you know?" I gasp.

"I had never drank much and I didn't drink that much then, but I blacked out and I couldn't remember what happened. I woke up in a stranger's apartment. I later found out that it was Thomas and his friends. He swore that nothing happened…only I had tearing."

"Tearing?" I ask.

"Yeah. You know, vaginal tearing," she says without missing a beat. "He swore that I just fell asleep and nothing happened."

"Did you go to the police?"

"Nothing like that had ever happened to me. I never knew. I've heard of women being hurt and I've heard of women being beat up by their boyfriends, but I never thought it could happen to me. When it did, I was so distraught, lost, and just uncertain of everything. I couldn't imagine going to the police and what would I even tell them? I guess I should have, but all I wanted to do was take a shower. All I wanted to do was just not have it happen."

"I'm really sorry," I say, leaning forward over her desk.

I put her hand in mine.

"What happened? What happened after that?" I ask.

Katherine exhales deeply, intertwining her fingers, and then saying, "I took a shower. I examined myself. I noticed that I had a small tear, not enough to warrant stitches. That night, some of the memories came back. Not clear ones, just guys all around me. I couldn't see their faces. It's hard to talk about it."

I look at her. If she's holding back tears, I can't tell, but I know that she's telling me the truth.

This is one of the hardest things she's ever gone through.

She doesn't know me well, but she's taking a chance. She saw something in me that she recognized in herself and in her relationship to Thomas, and she doesn't even know the half of it.

"*Why* are you telling me all this?" I ask.

"I want you to know who he is, even if I have no proof. Even if I won't tell people about it publicly. I saw you two together and he has his eye on you."

"It's not what you think." I sit back, putting my hands in my lap.

"What do you mean?" she asks. Now it's her turn to reach over the table for my hand.

"We were together for a while."

"You were?"

"Yeah. He didn't treat me very well. I wish I had taken him more seriously at the time. Kind of the usual bullshit: Putting me down, calling me sexist, terrible names, and making me feel bad about who I was as a person."

"Yeah. I'm sorry about that. What happened?"

Katherine flips her hair from one side to another. It's chestnut brown and looks like it'd been blow dried by an expert. Mine on the other hand falls a little bit flatter, without that luster and with a bunch of dry shampoo.

"What happened?" she asks again.

31

I run my finger over the smooth soft plexiglass of her table. It's made to look like glass and it's doing a great job at the masquerading. I like how white it is, how clean.

There's a little pop of color in the bottom of the marble pot interlaced with gold that's holding a small succulent.

I reach over and touch one of the leaves, wanting to disappear into it.

Having this conversation with someone who really understands where I'm coming from feels strange. Sydney knows the details, but as everyone who has ever been abused or hurt knows, most of the time you're embarrassed to talk about it.

It's not that you always feel like it's your fault, it's more like you just don't want to think about it. You just want to dissociate from the body that belonged to that man.

In this case, he didn't hurt me sexually, but the physical attack made me feel so shitty and so bad about myself. It made me feel like I'm not good enough, but the truth is that I'm too good for him.

I don't want to hold it back anymore. Since Katherine told me her truth, I figure I might as well tell her my secret.

"He punched me in my stomach on one occasion. He slammed my head in the wall on another," I say. "It was always during an argument. I can't remember about what now. I do remember his grip on my neck. I remember how much it hurt when my head collided with the wall. I remember the rage. The cold, dark rage in his eyes and how he could easily have kept his hand there a minute longer and took my life. He liked knowing that, too. When he let go, I could tell that he did it because he wanted to show me that he could kill me."

"God, that's messed up," Katherine says.

"Yeah, it is. No one knew we were dating when it happened. We never filled out that paperwork with HR. You never know when is a good time to do that. You want to make sure that you're serious because you don't want to go back and fill out more paperwork about your personal life, so we kind of kept it a secret at first. Then that happened and we broke up."

"I'm sorry," she says.

"I found out that he got a court reporter pregnant. He was seeing her for a while. Then we had the argument and he punched me, strangled me, hit my head against the wall, and it was over, but..."

"You didn't tell anyone?"

I shake my head and admit, "No."

I want to cry but no tears come to the surface and I just feel this general sense of malaise wash over me.

"Why didn't you tell anyone? Why didn't you make a report?"

"Why didn't *you*?" I snap back.

"I'm sorry. I didn't mean to accuse you of anything. It wasn't an accusation. I was genuinely interested."

"Yeah, I'm sorry, too," I say immediately, regretting the fact that I was rude.

It's a natural question and in the way she asked it, it wasn't an accusation at all.

"I don't know. I mean, I do know. That's a lie."

I bring my hand up to my forehead and rub it, then I rub my temples. A headache, quiet but steady at first, settles somewhere in the back before making its way to the front.

"He's a colleague. No one knew we were dating. He has a lot more friends than I do. I didn't want to be *that* girl. This is the whole problem with not enough women in the force," I say. "It's a boys' club. You know that they still go to the strip clubs, play golf, and do all of these men-only activities to form closer bonds. Who are *they* going to believe? Him, their buddy, their friend, or his crazy ex-girlfriend?"

"So-called crazy. Kind of reminds me of a quote by Margaret Atwood," Katherine says. "'*Men are afraid that women will laugh at them. Women are afraid that men will kill them.'"*

Silence fills the room. We listen to it together and apart, sharing our sadness and commiserating with one another.

"What now?" I ask.

"I think we have to play it by ear. I have a feeling that he's going to dig his own grave."

"Not quickly enough," I say.

"Totally, but with the way he got mad at Danny, hopefully Danny has enough sense to get himself an attorney to press charges against the department."

"That's not a really cool thing to say." I smile mischievously out of the corner of my lips. "I'm not sure what Captain Medvil will have to say about that."

"Actually, Captain Medvil would agree with us if he knew what Thomas Abrams did. The problem is that he doesn't know the truth and we're at fault for that as much as anyone else."

"You think we made the wrong decisions? You think we should have said something?"

"If I did, then I wouldn't be talking to you now," she tells me.

I walk out of her office knowing that I made a mistake not making a report against him before. My career would probably be over but at least there would be a paper trail of complaints.

I appreciate her coming to me.

I appreciate her telling me the truth about what happened because without her taking that chance, I wouldn't know the other part of who Thomas is and what he's capable of.

The thing is that people like this, they don't just do one thing and forget about it. It doesn't work like that. It's an escalation.

Somebody didn't stop him from groping her and didn't call attention to it in high school, so in college he slipped another girl a roofie and took advantage of her.

Maybe by the time he was a senior, he full on held her down and had his way.

I don't know the extent of his sexual history or what exactly he did or didn't do and the truth is that neither does Katherine.

Maybe he was there and watched, maybe he participated, but is it really so much worse to watch and not participate?

To stand there as a helpless girl gets raped by your friends?

Is that really okay?

There's a law on the books for which many young men are serving a lot of hard years in prison that says that it's not. If you're in the car while a robbery takes place, it doesn't even matter if you're the getaway driver or not.

It doesn't matter if your friends told you that they were going to be hitting up a liquor store or maybe did it just in the spur of the moment for fun.

The only thing that matters is that, if somebody gets killed in the commission of that crime, you're as much at fault for what they did as they are.

If it applies to stealing money from a convenience store, shouldn't the same apply to sexual assault?

I don't make it far down the hallway when I hear footsteps behind me.

"Hey. Hey, Kaitlyn. Wait up." Katherine catches up to me and hands me my phone. "You forgot this."

"Oh, thanks. Sorry."

"Listen, I just want to let you know that I heard about your sister."

I shake my head, uncertain as to what to say.

"I'm really sorry. I'm going to look into it. I don't know what I can do, but I can make some calls if you want."

I shrug and sadly admit, "Right now it's all about canvassing the neighborhood. The deputies up there have already done it, but they haven't found out much so I'm just going to head back and ask more questions."

"Sounds like a good plan." She shifts her weight from one foot to another.

"Listen, I really appreciate you saying that," I say. "I'll definitely take you up on it in the future. God knows I'll probably need your help."

"Of course. How long has it been?"

I bite my lip. I don't want to say the exact number of days even though the number's ingrained in my mind.

"Too long."

"I'm really sorry."

"Her friend just went missing under similar circumstance. The FBI is working on it now."

"Really?"

"Yeah, but there's no evidence. They found their clothes packed into these bags all folded up and nice but nothing came back from CSI yet so I have no idea."

I lean closer to her.

I don't want to say this part too loudly.

It's almost as if the words are too scary to utter at full volume. "I think the case has gone cold."

"Don't say that," Katherine whispers.

"I don't want to but that's just what it feels like. There are not any leads. It's like they both vanished into thin air. I had some hope when Natalie went missing. Maybe if they were looking for two girls instead of one there'd be more of a chance to find them, but no, doesn't seem like that."

"*Someone* has to know something. Don't get down, stay proactive."

I nod. I appreciate her urgency and confidence.

"Just keep asking questions. Her friends. Their parents. Any random comments and statements. Out loud or on social media. Kids, they post everything."

"Yeah, I know." I nod.

"You're going to find her… alive," Katherine promises me.

She takes my hand in hers, pulls me close, and gives me a warm hug.

A tear runs down my cheek. I let myself sob like I haven't in a while. She wraps her arm around my shoulder and makes me feel like I'm not alone.

32

When it begins to rain, I decide to drive back home. I throw a few things into a bag, make sure that I have all my electronics and plugs, and I drive through the sad LA drizzle.

Los Angeles is beautiful when it's sunny and bright. Then the sky doesn't have a single cloud and beams with turquoise.

On overcast days, especially when you're driving on a freeway through the eastern parts, everything is gray, dark, and concrete.

I get tired of music and instead put on an audio book, while I wait in traffic of cars stacked like matchboxes. The narrator's voice drones on and somehow matches up with the sound of the rain hitting the windshield.

A tragedy unfolds in the story, horrific, but not scary. It's a thriller, a mystery, and unknown. I usually stay away from books like this because I have enough of that in my real life, but I liked the way she sounded in the sample.

I liked the whole anti-social aspect to it. Sometimes I'm attracted to books like *Gone Girl*, where you have an anti-hero telling the story. If I let myself think too much and I let myself go too much into my own mind, that's what happens to me. My thoughts can be quite dark and macabre.

I can blame it on my job and all the ugliness that I see in the world, but the truth is that it's something else. I've always felt this way, particularly on those dark dreary days.

It's hard to get out of bed.

It's hard to do anything productive.

It's hard to even care.

Driving a car, however, is not particularly hard. It's all become automatic now. I let myself drift off and space out. I lose myself in my thoughts and my body keeps taking me further and further away from my apartment and closer to a place I used to call home.

I have a few days here.

I'm not sure how many exactly, but Captain Medvil wants Danny to have some days to cool off. He wants him to think about everything that had happened in the interrogation and all the lies that he told.

He wants him to talk to his fiancée, Eve, and try to think of a story. This is a common tactic. We want Danny to get nervous, to worry about what he may or may not have told us.

The thing is that we don't have any evidence to arrest him. So, unless he comes forward and tells us exactly where Nick is, we don't have much of a case.

I have some suspicions, but not anything that will lead to the courtroom.

When I get to Big Bear, snow begins to fall. Small little flurries start to circle and the temperature begins to drop.

Instead of heading straight home, I stop by to talk to Lynn Wrasel, a student in Violet's art class. She's one of the many girls on my list that I want to speak with.

I saw Violet in a picture on her Instagram page. The caption on it talked about how much they loved art together and how much Lynn misses her friend.

I've never heard Violet mention her name before.

It doesn't mean much, but because I don't know every one of her friends and everyone that she had spoken to, I wish that we were closer as sisters.

I wish that I was someone that she could confide in, but I'm eighteen years older. She knows me more as an adult than a friend, but I was also someone who was too busy with my own personal life, career, and drama to pay as much attention to her.

Lynn Wrasel lives in one of the apartments by a waterfront in Big Bear Lake. There aren't many apartment buildings in this area, but these are one of the newer structures.

Most are condos rented out by rich Los Angelenos on short-term rental sites. I find out that her mom doesn't own this place because when I looked up the property records, somebody else is listed on the deed.

When I called earlier, Mrs. Wrasel had agreed to the interview, but said that she wants to be present. I'm hoping that once Lynn becomes a little bit more comfortable with me, we can talk in private.

Mrs. Wrasel, or Mindy, as she asks me to call her, has big kind eyes and a short layered haircut. She's wearing scrubs because she's a nursing assistant at the local hospital.

Her neck is draped in jewelry and a little rose tattoo is peeking out from underneath the sleeve of her left arm. From the looks of it, it appears to be quite intricate and well done. The rose is wrapped around a dagger puncturing something.

I'm about to say something about it, but Mindy pulls down her sleeve, clearly not interested in discussing it. Lynn comes out of her room and waves hello.

I take a brief look at the second floor condominium. There's only one source of light coming from the big window all the way across the living room, but it's also partially blocked by a patio.

Mindy waves me over to sit down on the futon masquerading as a couch in the living room and asks me how they can help me.

"You have such a nice view," I say, looking out onto the lake.

The flurries have morphed into more substantial snowflakes, heavy and wet.

They swirl around and land on the railing. It's already dark outside, but I'm familiar with the style of apartments and they are usually dim even on the brightest days due to the stacking of the patios one on top of the other.

"I'm really sorry about your sister," Lynn says, cracking her knuckles.

She's slim and tall. The strands of hair bordering her face are dyed fuchsia pink. It's actually a nice look. They frame her face in a way and bring out the paleness of her skin.

Her nails are painted a dark maroon color and peeling off in parts. The nails are short and I doubt that they're acrylic. The manicure itself looks rather homemade.

I ask Lynn about Violet and how she knew her. I mention that I saw her post on Instagram.

"We weren't like super close, but we had art together."

"Do you like it?" I ask.

"Yes, very much. We worked on a papier-mâché project together. Her favorite was doing these black and white sketches. I actually took pictures of some."

She pulls out her phone and scrolls through her camera roll. She shows me the skull, dagger, and two roses framing the picture in both ends.

"Violet did this?" I ask.

She nods.

"I've never seen her draw anything like this."

"Yeah. I don't know," she says, shrugging her shoulders. "She's been really getting into these kinds of images. Did you see her other Instagram page?"

"Her other one?" I ask.

"Yeah, the one that's devoted to her art."

I shake my head and admit, "No. I never even knew she had another account."

She pulls it up and I see the name at the top: *Violet Paige Art*. Paige is her middle name.

I swallow hard. The page is populated with artwork resembling death, suffering, and darkness. There are ravens, skulls, cemetery scenes, and even zombies eating brains.

The dominant colors in all the pictures seem to be black, red, and gray with accents of yellow.

"Okay, I know this looks really dark," Lynn says, "but let me explain."

I nod.

"She was really into reading about horror. You know that, right?"

I nod, even though I don't know anything about that.

"Like Stephen King and Christopher Pike."

I nod. Christopher Pike was one of my favorites when I was growing up.

"So, it's not like she's disturbed, even though her artwork sort of looks like it."

I nod, trying to believe her.

"You're convinced?" Lynn says, pulling on her spaghetti strap after it drops down off her shoulder.

She's dressed in black jeans, a tight belly button showing black tank top with spaghetti straps and a flannel t-shirt. I swear that I'm back in the nineties.

"She didn't want your mom to know this," she says, leaning over to me.

Mindy sits at the dining room table with a laptop in front of her pretending to be busy, but by the way that her head moves, I can tell that she's actively listening.

"Here, come to my room," Lynn says, catching her mom spying on us.

"Sorry!" Mindy yells a half-hearted apology.

"Does it matter," Lynn says, waving her hand.

Her mom's room is right across the way and it looks like a page out of an IKEA catalog while Lynn's is the kind of bedroom you'd expect a teenager in a movie to have.

The walls are painted black and one side is covered entirely in pictures cut out from magazines. It looks like at one point it was a collage and then it became something else entirely: just faces, a crowd of people looking at you.

A string of lights hangs above her bed and instead of a nightstand, she has a small white desk, which is cluttered with papers, art projects, binders, and a laptop.

Lynn opens the bottom drawer of her desk and pulls out a folder.

"She made these recently," she says and hands them to me.

I look through the drawings and the paintings inside. More skulls, more daggers, and more cemetery scenes, but the style is evolving. The details are becoming brighter. Some of them are from the pictures posted on the Instagram page.

"Why do you have these?" I ask.

She shakes her head.

"Why do you have these?" I ask again.

She looks down at the floor while whispering, "She told me to hold onto them. She didn't want your mom to find them."

"Why?"

"She was really not supportive of her art. She didn't want her to go to that art school in LA. Please don't tell her about the Instagram page. If ... when Violet comes back," Lynn says, correcting herself, "I don't want her to know that I was the one that exposed her secret."

Violet's art school dream is familiar to me. She told me all about it the one week she stayed in my apartment, trying to get some space from Mom after a particularly bad fight.

"So, she was just drawing this dark art? I don't know why Mom would have a problem with that."

"She wasn't just drawing the stuff," Lynn says.

I wait for her to explain. She licks her lips, bites the inside of her cheek, and then finally brings her bright blue eyes to mine.

"She was tattooing these images on people and herself."

I stare at her, uncertain if I heard her correctly.

"How can she tattoo anyone? You're not even allowed in a tattoo shop until you're eighteen." I shake my head, not wanting to believe her.

Lynn nods and says, "She had a machine and everything. She was mainly doing them on herself."

33

I'm not sure how to react to what Lynn told me.

This is wholly unexpected, but is it really that crazy? A lot of people have tattoos, but I've never heard of a pre-teen girl doing them, let alone on other people.

"How did she get into this?" I ask.

"She always liked to draw and then watched this show called *Ink Master,*" Lynn says, licking her lips. "That was just this revelation. She was like, 'Wow, tattooing isn't just for bikers and old, scary men.' She tried it out. She made those designs, like the skull and the flowers, and she kept working on them. Then she started watching all of these YouTube videos about how to do them on yourself because she couldn't get an apprenticeship anywhere."

"She couldn't?" I ask.

Lynn hesitates and the way that she recoils from the question tells me that there's a good chance she's lying.

"Okay, I'm going to tell you something, but you really can't tell anyone."

I nod.

This is something that people say a lot, but what do they expect me to do? I have to talk to the person to confirm the story.

I don't think that Lynn realizes any of this, but I want her to keep talking for as long as possible.

She swallows hard and finally says, "Violet couldn't get an apprenticeship anywhere and it's really hard to learn how to tattoo if someone doesn't really show you. YouTube videos only go so far."

"So, what did she do?"

"She went around to all the local shops and a bunch of them told her to go to hell. I mean, she looks young and she has a fake ID, but..."

"She has a fake ID?" I ask.

"Well, she got one to try to get this job, but it didn't really work except for the last place that she went to, Mile High Tattoo. It's out in Big Bear City. It's kind of out of the way and it's like a two person place. They told her to come over and they'd show her a few things."

"So, she was working there?"

"We had a deal where whenever she went there, she would tell her mom that she was coming *here*."

"How did she get there?"

"She took the bus."

I shake my head and state, "I can't believe that they let her into that place."

"Yeah. Well, the guy who owns it, his little brother is in eleventh grade and kind of knows her from school."

"You're in eighth grade," I say.

"Cameron knows everyone." Lynn laughs.

"What's his last name?" I ask.

"Shapinsky."

"As in Mr. Shapinsky?" I ask.

"Yeah, he's the chemistry teacher." She nods.

"Wow."

"Do you know him?" she asks.

I immediately have a flashback to the stern, no-nonsense teacher that never accepted any of my excuses for turning in late work. He was obsessed with keeping the Erlenmeyer flask clean and the Bunsen burner had to be used just right. If you used the wrong flask for the wrong thing to do your chemical reaction, you lost a lot of points.

I pace around her room, looking at all the paintings. I'm trying to figure out how I could have missed all of this.

I was so focused on talking to Neil, Natalie, and then her brothers that I completely ignored a whole other part of her life.

"Listen, I should have come forward earlier, but the cops came around and they asked me these questions."

"So, someone asked you? Someone came here and talked to you?"

"They talked to everyone at the school, almost everyone, I guess, but I was shy and I didn't want to get in trouble. I only really wanted to tell you. I'm really sorry."

"I wish you had said something earlier. We lost a lot of time," I say.

Lynn starts to choke up.

A tear runs down her cheek and she begins to sob. I suddenly feel bad.

I know that she's just a young girl who has no idea what she's doing. She's just pretending to be an adult, just like the rest of them.

"So, Cameron is a junior and you know him from school?"

"Yeah. He would hang out around the playground and we kind of saw him around."

"Saw him around, why? What was he doing?"

She shrugs and wipes her tears.

I let her get herself composed. I look around at some of the paintings on the walls. The one that is the most striking is the big dolphin jumping out of the water.

Unlike Violet's work, Lynn's paintings are light and bright. They look like they are actually done by a middle schooler, rather than a twenty-year-old biker who just got out of prison.

"You're very talented," I say. "Yeah, I really like this dolphin. I notice that you have a lot of ocean life."

She pulls her hair up into a bun on top of her head. Lynn sits down at her desk, spinning around on the swivel chair to face me. She looks small, delicate, and hurt.

"Please tell me everything that you know, even if it's illegal or improper. I'm her sister," I plead. "I just need to find her and I need to know everything in order to do that. As a detective, I can tell you that a clue can be any insignificant thing. You may not think it's important, but when we start to connect the dots, each of those dots is super important."

"Cameron sells a lot of weed," she says, shrugging her shoulders. "He's a drug dealer. He's very good and everyone likes him. He usually has really good stuff."

"Thank you." I nod.

I was half suspecting that. That's why he hangs out by schools.

"Is Violet... into drugs?" I ask, trying to be very careful with my words.

"I wouldn't say that. I mean, there's people who get high at like seven in the morning, but we just smoked a few joints once in a while, like at parties and stuff."

"Did you buy them from Cameron?"

She nods.

"You said that his older brother is the one who owns the tattoo shop?"

"Yeah. He went to art school in LA and then dropped out so his dad paid for him to open that tattoo shop. He has a lot of friends and knows the locals. He's actually kind of active on social media. So, he's got some clients from LA as well."

"What about Violet? What is their relationship?"

34

Lynn pulls her feet up to her chest and looks away from me. I pull my chair a little bit closer to her.

"Violet was looking for a shop to teach her to how tattoo. Everyone said no. She talked to Cameron and he got his brother to kind of agree to it."

I ask, "To what exactly?"

"To letting her apprentice. She was mainly doing a lot of the cleaning and setting up. Then she could also hang out and see how it worked and how everything was done."

"What about my mom?"

"She didn't know anything about it."

"Are you sure?" I ask.

"Yeah. I'm certain."

"Why do you say that?"

"Well, we were friends and I was the place that she was going to be when she was getting the tattoos."

I nod, taking it all in.

"You mentioned that she had tattoos and she started tattooing people?"

"Yeah. She's been working there for about half a year now. She was getting quite good. Here."

Lynn pulls out her phone again from her back pocket and shows me another Instagram page. This one is called Violet Paige Tattoos.

She starts to scroll through.

There are hundreds of pictures. My mouth nearly drops open. Most are replicas from the artwork that I've seen on the other page and in the folder, but there are some other ones, ones that don't seem to fit.

One looks like the dolphin that's hanging on the wall.

"This one looks like yours." I point to it.

She nods.

"Did she do this tattoo?"

"Yeah. On me."

"Wow. Where?"

She pulls up her shirt and I see a big dolphin jumping over her hip bone.

"This is beautiful."

The work is outlined perfectly and has amazing shading. The water droplets look so real that the dolphin looks wet. It has a little smile and it glistens in the sun.

"This looks so real," I say.

She nods.

"I love it. Is this the only one that she did?"

"Yeah. She started working on another one, but we didn't get that far. It was going to go on my back."

"Your mom is okay with this?"

"Violet is the one who did the rose and dagger on her forearm."

"Really?" I gasp.

"Yeah. She was actually one of her first real customers. My mom has a number of other tattoos, so she didn't see what the big deal was."

I nod.

It's suddenly dawning on me just how little I knew my sister.

"What about my mom?"

"Your mom was really against tattoos," Lynn says as if she's reading my mind. "She's just... Violet told me all of these horrible things she said. The few times that Violet jokingly brought up getting one, your mom freaked out."

I nod. That sounds about right.

"Do you have any?" Lynn asks, walking over and reaching for my hand.

I shake my head.

"Never wanted one?"

"I wouldn't say that, but when I was growing up, it was more taboo, I guess you could say. It was just something that a lot of men had and that tattoos weren't very attractive. I thought about getting one in college like a butterfly or some stars on my back, but I don't know. I could never commit."

"Violet said that a lot of tattoo artists have a lot of crappy tattoos but it doesn't really matter because they each tell a story. They're all memories."

We walk out to the kitchen where Mindy continues to sit at the dining room table covered with books and an open laptop.

"I'm getting my bachelor's degree," she explains. "I want to go to medical school."

That takes me by surprise. "Really?"

"Yeah. Actually, Violet really encouraged me. I always wanted to be a doctor, but then I got pregnant and had to raise a child on my own. So, working in the medical field was the best that I could do, but now that my daughter is growing up and needs a little bit less supervision, why not?" Mindy smiles. "It will take me four years to get my bachelor's degree, maybe more, and then who knows? Maybe I can go to med school."

"That's great. I hope you do," I encourage her.

Slowly blood rushes away from her face.

"What? What did I say?" I ask.

She swallows hard, then forces herself to look at me and say, "The way you said it. You just sounded so much like Violet. We really miss her. She was like family. She was like my other kid."

"Lynn told me that you let her tattoo you."

"It's so special to have her artwork on my arm."

I nod and suddenly realize that both of them here have something of Violet's that I will never have unless I find her again.

They have a memento that's stronger than a photograph. It's part of them. It's ingrained on their skin.

Every time they look at it, they can be with her.

"You're going to find her, right?" Lynn says.

"Yes, of course. I'm going to do everything I can and the next thing I want to do is talk to Cameron."

"Please don't tell him that I was the one that told you. He's kind of a connected guy, you know? I don't want to get hurt."

"Of course not. Your secret is safe with me."

I walk downstairs and instead of going to the parking lot to my car, I head toward the waterfront.

There's a small park with a playground to the left and then a boat launch. The lake is mostly marsh upfront due to a series of droughts over many years, but this winter has gotten a lot of precipitation, so the marshy part is covered by water.

I walk down the rocky path to get as close to the shore as possible. The wind picks up and I pop my collar wishing that I had a hat.

I'm not going to stay out here long, but I need to take this place in for just a little bit longer, because this is where Violet spent a lot of happy time.

This is where she could be her true self.

I'm just sorry that she wasn't that way at home or with me.

35

I go by the tattoo shop, but it's closed. The sign upfront says they'll be open at nine the following morning and I plan to be there by at least eight thirty.

Night has settled in now and the flurries continue to fall. I debate whether I should head straight to my mom's house who doesn't know that I'm coming or stop by and see Luke at the hotel.

There are so many things that we have left unresolved. He asked me to be more serious with him and I told him no, but I don't even know why.

The truth is that I want that.

I knock on the door of his room, second floor up, with a wind gusting off the lake and hitting me straight in the face.

He can't open it fast enough and when he does, I give him a big hug.

At first, he's surprised, but after a moment, he embraces me back and pulls me into the room.

I shut the door with my boot and I hold him for a while.

"What's wrong? What happened?"

"Nothing." I shake my head. "I just missed you."

"I missed you, too," he says, kissing the top of my forehead and then going down my cheek, eventually finding my mouth.

We hold each other for a few moments, locked in our kiss and everything seems to be okay.

I haven't met someone I could talk to like this for a long time. I feel like I can tell him anything and he would understand where I'm coming from without judging me.

I take off my jacket and sit down on the edge of the bed. I rub my hands together to warm up.

I spent half an hour walking the lake shore after I talked to Lynn Wrasel, trying to piece all of Violet's secrets together into one cohesive unit. That's the thing about secrets, they don't always make sense.

People are contradictions of themselves. The person you know is a face and a version of themselves, but there are many versions of them.

It doesn't mean that they are liars, not necessarily. Some people are.

In Violet's case, I think she was just keeping certain things to herself because she didn't think that anyone would understand or care to understand.

"It's Violet's birthday," I say, my voice cracking. "She's fourteen today."

"Oh, of course. Yes. I saw that in the paperwork."

Luke sits down on the edge of the bed with me and drapes his hand over my shoulder as I start to tell him everything that I found out from Lynn and her mom and about this whole other life that my sister led.

"Tattoos, huh?" Luke shakes his head.

"I mean, that's not that horrible, right? It's not like she was into drugs."

"No, it's not."

"I think she was mainly doing it for art, but knowing my mom, she wouldn't understand. She's pretty open about some things and then others, she's just locked in her views. For her, tattoos are for bikers, criminals, and prisoners, not for sweet little girls. That's probably why Violet never told her anything about it. I just wish that she opened up to me."

He nods his head softly.

"The thing is that I wasn't worth her honesty. I wasn't a good sister, not for the last six months or so. I was so busy with my promotion, with all of these cases, I was consumed with work and still am."

"Don't you see that this obsession is going to help you find her? You don't give up, Kaitlyn. Maybe that's what pushed you two apart," Luke says softly, patting my back. "That's also what's going to bring her home."

We sit here in the damp room with deep blue carpeting and a light blush pink jacuzzi tub in the corner. The carpet goes all the way to the edge, so if any water spills out or when you step out of it, the area right in front gets soggy and wet.

It's not a good look, but the room is otherwise clean and well kept up.

I feel the tub calling me.

"I have to tell you something," Luke says when I reach over to kiss him.

He pulls away just before our lips touch and the serious expression on his face puts my stomach into knots.

"I don't want to hear anything bad," I say. "Not now."

I reach over and kiss him again.

His hand slides underneath my shirt. "Not unless you tell me that you have a girlfriend or you're married or something like that."

"No, it's nothing like that," he mumbles, pressing his lips to mine. "Well, let's talk about it after."

After we make love, he holds me for a long time. I press my naked body against his, snuggling up, and he wraps his legs around mine, draping his arms over my shoulders.

For a moment, I forget who I am and I'm just Kaitlyn Carr, a woman falling for Luke Gavinson, the man that she's been looking for a long time and only recently found.

We lie under a single sheet, letting the warmth of our bodies heat each other up. The chill of the night quickly covers us and it's not enough.

"Have you used the hot tub?" I ask.

"Yeah."

"How was it?"

"Not as nice as it's going to be." He smiles at me and even though I can't see it, I can feel it, and it warms my heart.

He walks over to the tub, flips it on, and a rush of water starts to geyser out.

The tub seems bigger than it is because it doesn't take that long for it to fill. Luke climbs in first and I watch as his sculpted, lean body descends under the water.

Suddenly, I feel a little shy, even though the room is lit up by one faint light bulb from the nightstand, which resembles a candle.

I'm self-conscious about my body as I make my way across the room, but when our eyes meet, I start to relax.

"You are breathtaking," he says.

Licking his lips, Luke reaches out for my hand to help me in. I descend into the water, watching the ripples spread in between us and I sit across from him, moving slightly to the side to avoid the faucet.

"Thank you for coming here," he says. "I've missed you."

"I've missed you, too."

I rub my foot along the outside of his hip flexors. I remember that he had something to tell me, some bad news, but I can't force myself to bring it up.

Not right now.

I didn't want to hear it earlier and I certainly don't want to hear it now. I've had enough bad news to last a lifetime and right now I need something good to hold on to.

A few minutes later, just as I put my head back, close my eyes, and feel grateful for everything that I do have, my phone goes off.

I want to ignore it, but I wonder who would be calling me at this hour. My mom would only call if it were an emergency.

I climb out of the water, wrap a towel around myself to not drip so much water onto the carpet, and reach for my phone.

"Eve?" I answer almost immediately after seeing her name pop on the screen.

"Detective Carr. Kaitlyn." Her voice sounds faint.

There's a lot of sound in the background.

Luke turns on the water to fill up the hot tub with a little bit more warm water, but I motion for him to turn it off.

"Eve, what's going on?" I say loudly, pressing the phone to my ear. It occurs to me that it may be good for Luke to hear as well so I put her on speakerphone.

"You have to help me," Eve whimpers.

36

The sound of the road is hard to deny. I can hear people beeping as the car moves swiftly down the freeway.

"Danny Usoro put me in my trunk. He's driving," she says in a loud whisper.

"What's your license plate number?" I ask, grabbing a notepad and a pen.

She rattles it off and I'm actually surprised that she knows it by memory.

"Honda Civic 2007!" she yells, her voice becoming more confident.

"What happened?"

"I don't know. He hit me with something. My head is bleeding and then I woke up here in the trunk. I didn't know where I was. He doesn't know that I have my phone."

"I'm going to put out an APB. Going to get you some help, Eve. We're going to find you. Do you have any idea where he's going?"

"No," she whimpers. "He just came over. We were talking and he got all mad. He said that you're going to find out the truth and there's nothing he can do. I told him that he needs to get a lawyer and I kept asking him what he did. Then he hit me. Everything is blurry."

"Okay, stay calm, please stay calm," I urge her when she starts to sound like she's hyperventilating.

I glance over at Luke, who's already making the calls. I hear him put out an all-points bulletin, APB for short, for her car, giving her description.

I keep her on the line as we get dressed.

I keep her talking.

I don't dare hang up. You never hang up.

She tells me how frustrated he looked, how scared, and how she wanted to ask him about what happened to Nick and Janine, but she was too afraid.

"That was the first time that I really thought that he had something to do with her murder and his disappearance," she whispers and begins to sob.

I pull on my pants and button my shirt.

I put on my coat and boots and grab my keys, all while talking to her. The LA Sheriff's Department and the LAPD are going to look for her, but I have to as well.

Luke puts her number into an app on his phone and it shows that they're traveling east on I-10. We get into the car.

I keep asking her about where he might be taking her and why is she in the trunk.

She says she doesn't know, and she cries when she tells me that her legs are bound with zip ties and so are her hands. The only reason why she was able to call me was because he bound them in the front.

"Oh my God! The car's slowing down," she whispers.

I hear the sound of the wheels in the background. It sounds like they are pulling off on an exit.

"Stay calm. Please stay calm."

"No, I have to go. I can't. He can't find out that I have this phone on me. I have to put it back. If I don't see you again-"

"Don't think like that, Eve. We're going to find you. I'm going to find you. Everything's going to be fine."

She hangs up before I can finish. I stare at the screen for a few moments, sitting in the front passenger seat as Luke takes us down the mountain.

He's driving so fast that the snow collides with the windshield and creates a warp effect in the headlights.

My head spins.

"Put on your seat belt." I finally hear Luke saying somewhere in the distance.

I reach over and buckle myself in. "Here, take my phone. You can see where they're going."

"You have an app that tracks phone numbers?"

"Yeah, iPhones that have their locations on."

I call dispatch and confirm the APB. The woman on the other end tells me that it looks like the car's heading to the Ontario Airport long-term parking lot.

I see the same thing on Luke's app and my heart sinks. We're still half an hour away, at least.

"We're not going to make it," I say, rubbing my temples and folding myself in half because my stomach starts to hurt. "We're too far away. If we don't make it, somebody else will."

The road gets slicker and slicker while the snowfall gets more intense. They're not that many people out on the roads, but at one point when we making a turn, we slip and roll into oncoming traffic, swerving just in time.

"We have to get down this mountain safely," Luke says, grabbing the steering wheel tighter.

A little bit later, we finally arrive. I check the location of the phone again and it's still there.

"What do you think is happening?" I ask.

"I don't know. I haven't heard anything."

When we pull up, there are flashing lights and a couple of police cars near the entrance of the parking structure.

The Honda Civic is in the long-term lot, apart from the other cars.

The trunk is empty, but her phone is laying right there in the center. He's onto us.

"What does this mean?" Luke asks, not really asking me in particular.

"He couldn't have gone that far," I say.

"Not on foot anyway."

"He probably had a backup car here," I say.

Now, we have no idea what vehicle he's driving and Eve no longer has a phone.

I swallow hard and shift my weight from one foot to another nervously. Suddenly, I realize that I'm sweating.

The jacket is way too warm for this tepid valley air. Even though it's snowing up on the mountain, down here the temperature hovers in the mid-sixties.

I pull off my hat and gloves and unzip my coat, letting the scarf fall loosely around my neck.

"What do we do now?" Luke asks.

───────────

THE SHERIFF's department stays behind to process the scene, pick up fingerprints, or find any other evidence that's available from the trunk.

Luke and I get back in the car and try to figure out what to do. He starts the engine and begins to drive.

Sometimes it's easier to think like this.

Where would you go?

What would you do?

The problem is that I don't know Danny very well.

There were certain things pointing to him as someone who had possible involvement, but what does that mean exactly?

I thought that maybe he was just covering for his friend, Nick, but why would he take Eve as hostage?

Why would he put her in the trunk?

Why would he overreact to such an extreme degree if he didn't have anything to do with this?

Luke drives slowly to the parking lot. Going down the various levels in the structure, we reach the second floor, turning right instead of left to get to the next level.

"Where are you going?" I ask.

"I just thought that I'd check out the parking lot."

"You think that there might be a chance that he's here?" I ask.

"I have no idea."

Luke makes his way around, seeing nothing and then drives up one more level just in case.

In the corner, right around the side of the elevators, we see a figure standing in the shadows, sitting on the floor, shaking.

"That's them." I gasp and reach for my weapon.

We have to be careful. We have no idea what he has on him.

"Please don't shoot him. We have to try to take him in."

He nods.

I know that if there's anyone I can trust with that, it would be Luke. If Thomas were here, I wouldn't be so cavalier about it.

Thomas doesn't follow all of the police academy's rules, but the one he does like is shoot first and ask questions later.

Luke pulls over.

We immediately swing our doors open and shield ourselves behind them. We're close enough for him to hear when I identify myself.

"Danny, this is the police!" I yell.

"And the FBI!" Luke yells. "Put your weapon down."

"No, I don't think so!" Danny yells back.

37

Eve whimpers loudly.

He presses the barrel into her head. She yelps. There's a small light above Danny's head that casts shadows and lets me see a little bit of what's going on as he moves.

"What do you want to do?" I whisper to Luke.

"There's a staircase right over there," he mutters.

I nod.

"If you distract him, I can make my way up and around and surprise him on the other side," I offer.

"That's a big risk." He shakes his head.

"You know what's going to happen when backup arrives. He'll end up dead and he might take her with him."

"No, it's too dangerous. I don't want you to go."

"That's not up to you," I say, checking my weapon. "Just keep talking to him. Take control and make him think that you're the main negotiator."

"If you surprise him, he might shoot her," he hisses at me.

Luke's eyes narrow.

I lick my lips to realize how chapped they are and how desperate I am for a gulp of water. Even a little sip would do.

My headache builds in momentum, but I force myself to stay focused.

I can't let myself get distracted in any way.

"What are you going to do when you get there?" Luke says.

"I don't know. I'm going to take my phone so you can hear me, okay?"

He nods.

I call him and Luke accepts. I put my cell in my front pocket so he can hear everything.

I glance across the parking lot.

If I walk straight across, Danny will see me. The floor is covered in big black shadows, so the only way that this will work is if I slither my way over to the staircase.

I get down on the ground.

The asphalt is dirty and smells of motor oil and sweat. I'm tempted to go on all fours, but I force myself to take my time and slide on my stomach.

Luke makes a racket to draw Danny's attention to him. He talks loudly, drops stuff on the floor, makes jokes.

I finally make it all the way to the exit sign when my palm lands in a pile of old vomit.

My face contorts, my gag reflex sets in, and I'm about to throw up. Pushing it back down, I wipe my hand off on the asphalt and keep going.

I finally rise to my feet and disappear into the staircase, running across the top level.

I take off my shoes right before I get to their staircase, to avoid making a loud clinking sound with my boots.

My feet feel the coldness of the cement, but I'm light on my feet, trying to imagine the movements of a ninja.

I make my way down to the first landing and hear Luke's voice. Peeking out just a little while pushing myself away from the wall, I see Eve sitting on the ground, her feet and hands bound up with her head in her knees.

She moves slightly, glancing back. Our eyes meet.

I bring my index finger to my lips to keep her quiet as her eyes become two big saucers with a glimmer of hope flickering in each.

Too bad, I don't really have a plan.

Danny has a 9mm in his right hand. He's holding onto it pretty firmly and I'm not sure what he will do if I startle him.

Some people react in fear, others in offense.

He may shoot out at Luke, who's not exactly in the position to shoot in this direction out of fear of hitting me or Eve. If he's particularly fast, he can quickly flip back and shoot me.

I consider what might happen if I press my weapon to the back of Danny's neck.

I don't want to shoot him, but if I do, I have to hit him center mass, the way that all police officers in this country are taught to shoot any armed or possibly armed suspect, no matter what.

But I want him alive.

So, I need to do something else.

While I hesitate, I take a step away, squashing a dried up leaf, which makes a loud crunching sound.

Danny turns around to look at me and our eyes meet. Just as I'm about to lift up my weapon, Eve stands up and slams her body into him, knocking him down to the ground.

I rush over and kick his gun away from his hand and point mine in his face, keeping distance so that he can't grab onto my legs to knock me down.

Everything happens in a flash. A moment later Luke is by my side, pointing his weapon in Danny's face.

38

After Danny is arrested, we find Nick's body in a storage unit across from the apartment. Nick had rented it only a few days before his death for Danny.

The front desk manager confirmed that both Danny and Nick were there when the agreement was signed. Danny talked about needing a place to store some stuff before a move, but it was rented in Nick's name because Danny didn't have enough credit.

I talk to Eve in the police station. The paramedics sew her head up and they don't find any internal bleeding or additional injuries at the hospital. Still, she remains a shell of the woman I had met earlier.

I find two additional blankets to wrap her up in, but she can't get any warmer. Her hands shake as she brings a cup of tea to her lips and her face has a faraway distant expression.

"Why did Danny do this?" I ask. "Why did he take you?"

She turns to look away, her eyes unable to focus.

"When he pulled me out of that trunk and found my phone, he just lost it. He started to sob and he said that I betrayed him, but I didn't. I never thought that he would do anything like this. I didn't even think he would ever raise his hand to me, let alone kill…"

I swallow hard and I give her time to think, breathe, and collect her thoughts.

"Did he tell you anything? What did he do? Why?"

"Yeah." She nods and looks down into her cup, watching the swirls as she stirs it a little bit. "He told me that he did it all for me. I couldn't believe it."

"What are you talking about?"

"I never asked him to do anything. You have to believe me." She leans closer.

I nod.

"Danny said that he got fired from his job two months ago and he didn't want to tell me because he didn't want to disappoint me," she whispers. "We were planning this wedding and everything was costing so much money. We had to put down all of these deposits. The last one he was kind of late on it, but I didn't think anything of it. The cake place called and when I called them back, the woman said that they had been paid. So, I never gave it another thought."

"Okay." I nod, processing and trying to figure out where this is going.

"Well, the thing is that it was the money that Nick lent him."

I grab onto the arm of the chair with one hand so tightly that my knuckles turn white.

She glances down and I immediately stop.

"So, what happened next?" I push her.

"What happened was that he lied to me about having a job and he didn't have any money."

"Really?"

"And Nick did. That's what Danny said when he tied me up with those zip ties by the elevator. He was sobbing." Her voice lowers and blood drains away from her face. "It sounded like a confession. It was right before you two showed up and I thought that he was going to kill me and himself right there."

"Is that what he was saying? That's what he was going to do?"

"Yeah." Tears roll down her cheeks, but she doesn't go to wipe them away. "Danny told me that it was going to be better this way. That we were going to die like martyrs, like Romeo and Juliet, but he was running out of time and that was why he took me. He wanted to tell me everything before it happened."

The room goes quiet.

She meets my eyes and nods.

"He killed Janine in order to frame Nick," Eve says. "Danny had already killed him and stashed his body in that storage unit. Then he used Nick's phone to text Janine and ask her to come over. Danny wrote that he was having an anxiety attack, which was something that happened often to Nick, and he couldn't sleep. They were friends and Danny knew that. He knew that Janine would come over. That's what he told me."

Eve shakes her head, holds onto her shoulders tighter, and wraps herself tighter in the blankets.

It's almost like she wants to disappear underneath them.

"Why? Why would he kill Nick?" I ask.

"Money. He had over fifty-thousand dollars saved from being overseas and that's exactly what we needed for the wedding. It's actually a lot more than what we needed, but he was going to take the other twenty grand and we were going to start a new life together. I was never supposed to know about it, but then you started snooping around."

"So why didn't that plan work out?" I ask.

"You brought him in for questioning and he knew that you were getting close. He knew that you were going to come talk to me and he was freaking out. I think that's why he took me."

39

A few days later we get confirmation from the forensics lab that Danny's DNA evidence was found in Nick's apartment. Nick has also been shot by the same weapon as Janine and we find it in a nearby storage cubby in the parking lot below Danny and Nick's apartment building.

Refusing to talk to a lawyer and trying to explain away the mounting evidence against him, Danny is officially charged in the murder of Nick Millian and Janine Sato.

The following Monday, he's in jail awaiting trial for kidnapping his fiancée and taking her hostage.

Katherine Harris is extremely pleased with the evidence that we have, but we're still a long way away from a trial date and a conviction even though the evidence is strong and hard to argue with.

"You did a good job," Captain Medvil says, stopping by my desk as I gather my things. "Why don't you take a few days off? Go up to the mountains and check on your sister."

"Thanks. That's exactly what I want to do."

While I was busy at work here, Luke investigated the tattoo shop and talked to Cameron, his father, and his brother who all denied the fact that Violet worked there.

They basically stonewalled him. I want to go back up there and get some more answers if possible.

My phone rings just as I'm about to get in the car.

It's Luke.

We have plans to meet up for dinner tonight and I can't wait to see him again after all this time apart.

After closing this case and passing it on to the prosecutor, I finally have something to celebrate.

"I can't do tonight," Luke says as I look at him closer over FaceTime.

"What are you talking about? Why?"

"They're calling me up north tonight. Three young boys are missing in California City. They need extra manpower."

"What about Violet and Natalie?"

He shakes his head.

"What about the tattoo shop and everything that you found out?"

"There's no evidence that she worked there. They're refusing to cooperate and the case is going cold."

"No, don't say that," I say, pointing my finger in his face. "It's not going cold." A cold case means we're giving up.

"Obviously, it's not officially cold, but there are no other leads. There's nowhere else to go. It has taken a back burner to new cases and my boss tells me I have to go to California City. What can I do?"

I shake my head. I need to get up there. I need to investigate whatever is going on. I need to find answers. Maybe talk to people who are only willing to talk to me.

"You should come up here and interview more of her friends. Maybe talk to the tattoo shop again," Luke suggests.

"It could be nothing." I shrug.

"It could be everything, but I can't stay," Luke says, shaking his head. "Let me just go to California City. I'll start working that case and I'll be in touch. Maybe I can get a few days off and drive back. I want to see you again."

"I want to see you, too," I whisper.

"Don't give up. There's always something to uncover."

I nod and hang up.

Later that evening when I am licking my wounds, so to speak, and drinking a little bit too much wine, celebrating the closing of the case all by myself, my phone rings. It's Lynn Wrasel, Violet's friend.

"Cameron's dead," she says almost immediately after I answer. "I went to talk to him again because he was lying to the FBI and he disappeared. His dad, Mr. Shapinsky, was freaking out. He came to talk to us. He went to the cops. They just found his body."

THANK YOU FOR READING! I hope you loved Detective Kaitlyn Carr's investigation. The next book in the Kaitlyn Carr series is GIRL TAKEN.

1-click GIRL TAKEN now!

Don't stop looking…

When her sister's friend is found dead, Detective Kaitlyn Carr knows that time is running out. Her sister has been missing for weeks and everyone is starting to believe that she's gone for good. **But Kaitlyn refuses to give up.**

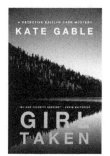 While the FBI and the Sheriff's investigators collect evidence and run tests, Kaitlyn stays busy with another case back in Los Angeles: the disappearance of a missing couple who were trying to sell their half a million dollar boat.

Their grown sons insist that their parents would have never left without an explanation, but it's up to Kaitlyn to uncover the truth.

Is the missing couple keeping secrets of their own or is their life actually in danger?

Who killed her sister's friend and will finding her killer lead to answers about Violet's disappearance?

1-click GIRL TAKEN now!

IF YOU ENJOYED THIS BOOK, please take a moment to write a short review on your favorite book site and maybe recommend it to a friend or two.

You can also join my Facebook group, Kate Gable's Reader Club, for exclusive giveaways and sneak peeks of future books.

WANT TO BE THE FIRST TO KNOW ABOUT MY UPCOMING SALES, NEW RELEASES AND EXCLUSIVE GIVEAWAYS?

Sign up for my newsletter:
https://www.subscribepage.com/kategableviplist

Join my Facebook Group:
https://www.facebook.com/groups/833851020557518

Bonus Points: Follow me on BookBub and Goodreads!

https://www.goodreads.com/author/show/
21534224.Kate_Gable

ABOUT KATE GABLE

Kate Gable loves a good mystery that is full of suspense. She grew up devouring psychological thrillers and crime novels as well as movies, tv shows and true crime.

Her favorite stories are the ones that are centered on families with lots of secrets and lies as well as many twists and turns. Her novels have elements of psychological suspense, thriller, mystery and romance.

Kate Gable lives in Southern California with her husband, son, a dog and a cat. She has spent more than twenty years in this area and finds inspiration from its cities, canyons, deserts, and small mountain towns.

Write her here:

Kate@kategable.com

Check out her books here:

www.kategable.com

Sign up for my newsletter:
https://www.subscribepage.com/kategableviplist

Join my Facebook Group:
https://www.facebook.com/groups/833851020557518

Bonus Points: Follow me on BookBub and Goodreads!

https://www.bookbub.com/authors/kate-gable

https://www.goodreads.com/author/show/
21534224.Kate_Gable

amazon.com/Kate-Gable/e/B095XFCLL7

facebook.com/kategablebooks

bookbub.com/authors/kate-gable

instagram.com/kategablebooks

ALSO BY KATE GABLE

All books are available at ALL major retailers! If you
can't find it, please email me at
kate@kategable.com

Girl Missing (Book 1)

Girl Lost (Book 2)

Girl Found (Book 3)

Girl Taken (Book 4)

Girl Hidden (FREE Novella)